SOMEWHERE TO CALL HOME

Patricia Lynn

ZEBRA BOOKS
KENSINGTON PUBLISHING CORP.

ZEBRA BOOKS are published by

Kensington Publishing Corp.
850 Third Avenue
New York, NY 10022

First Zebra Printing: June, 1996
10 9 8 7 6 5 4 3 2 1

Printed in the United States of America

One

"Mom, could we possibly be lost?"

"Heather, why do you always have to assume the worst?" Holly demanded. "I'm sure if Mom thought we were lost, she would have said so by now. Besides, the sign back on the main highway said Four Aces Ranch on it. It's got to be here somewhere."

Heather twisted around as far as her seat belt would allow and pinned her sister in the back seat with a frosty blue-eyed glare. "Well, take a look around. You can see for miles in any direction. Do you see a ranch out there anywhere?"

"No, but that doesn't mean anything. Things are not as close together in Montana as they are in Chicago."

Heather gave an exasperated groan and rolled her eyes. "No kidding, Einstein."

"Enough," Kathleen Hunter ordered, bringing instant silence from her two teenage daughters. She'd just about reached her limit for one day. She was exhausted, her head was pounding, and for all she knew, they could very well be lost.

Abruptly, she stopped the red mini van in the middle of the gravel road they were on and shifted it into park. Without a word of explanation, she shut the engine off and climbed out of the vehicle.

The dust the tires had stirred up drifted away on a lazy breeze. Kathleen stood a moment and looked back at the way they'd just come. Then she turned and gazed at the road ahead of them. As far as she could tell, there was absolutely nothing to distinguish the two directions. The road ribboned in both directions through rolling green meadows dotted with yellow and purple wildflowers before climbing subtly into sloping hillsides. Pine trees, standing tall and straight, were scattered about. And in the hazy distance blue mountains rose majestically into the sky. A warm June sun bathed everything in a golden glow.

Sighing, she leaned back against the van, giving no thought to the fact that she would now be wearing the thick dust covering the van on the backside of her jeans and shirt. Behind dark glasses her eyes closed as she allowed herself to be soothed by the tranquil sounds of nature around her.

"Mom!"

So much for tranquility. "Give me a break, Heather," she said wearily.

"There's someone coming," Holly called. "You better come around here."

By the time Kathleen rounded the van both girls were out of it. Holly pointed across a low valley. "He's coming this way."

Sure enough, a lone rider was moving steadily toward them. The horse and rider seemed to be one, and Kathleen was reminded of every John Wayne western she'd ever watched. With a kind of curious anticipation, she waited as the rider drew near.

When he reined the sleek black horse to a stop in front of them, the man tipped his hat slightly. "Good afternoon, ladies," he greeted, his voice deep, but void of the drawl Kathleen had been expecting. "Are you having problems with your van?"

"No," she said quickly. "We're on our way to the Four Aces Ranch. I was just beginning to wonder if I'd managed to take a wrong turn somewhere."

"You're okay," he assured her. "Keep on about another mile and you'll come to a fork in the road. Stay to the left. It'll take you right to the ranch. You can't miss it."

"Thank you." Kathleen wished she could see his eyes. The dusty Stetson on his head concealed his eyes as effectively as sunglasses. She wondered if she'd find any warmth in those eyes since none showed in the hard features of his face. Except his mouth. There was something oddly vulnerable about his lower lip that mocked the stern lines of his mouth. If he was at all curious about three females in the middle of nowhere, he didn't show it.

"Are you really a cowboy?" Heather issued this challenge, her blue eyes squinting as she tipped her head back to study him.

"Are you really a twin?" he returned smoothly.

Holly giggled and slid her sister a smug look. "He's got you there, Heather."

"Yeah, but it's obvious we're twins," she pointed out logically.

"Isn't it obvious I'm a cowboy?" Leather creaked as he shifted in his saddle. "I've got a cowboy hat and cowboy boots. I'm riding a horse named Lightning. I've got a rifle over here on the side." He shrugged lightly. "I must be a cowboy."

"Yeah, but are you a real cowboy?" Heather persisted in her usual manner. "Or are you just one of those pretend cowboys that Uncle Jon has on his dude ranch?" She pronounced the last two words with obvious disdain.

"Oh, I'm a real cowboy," the man assured her. "We don't give guns to the pretend ones."

Kathleen thought she saw a slight softening in the firm line of his mouth, as if a smile might have played there. But it came and went so quickly she couldn't be sure.

"Okay, but. . . ."

"That's enough, Heather," Kathleen interrupted. "Give the man a break. I'm sure he's got better things to do than stay here and argue with you." She looked up at him. "Thanks for the directions."

In response, he tilted his head slightly. "Have a nice day, ladies." With a slight tug on the reins the horse was wheeled around and started back the way they'd come.

Kathleen and the girls stood and watched as the graceful pair disappeared over a low ridge.

"Some cowboy," Holly murmured with awed appreciation.

"He's old," Heather said bluntly. "Probably close to forty."

"I don't care how old he is, he looks great on a horse. Maybe he has a son."

"Well, you can have him," Heather returned. "The last thing I want is a cowboy."

Kathleen sighed deeply and looked over at her two fourteen-year-old daughters. "Let's move on," she suggested. "If the cowboy wasn't lying, we should be close to the ranch."

"Oh, he wouldn't lie," Holly rushed to defend him. "He's a good guy."

"Oh, please," Heather muttered as she pulled the door open and climbed into the van.

Kathleen smiled slightly, taking in Holly's earnest expression and wide, innocent eyes. "Okay," she conceded softly. "He's a good guy. Let's go."

Holly followed her sister into the van as Kathleen walked around to the driver's side. Not for the first time, she wondered how God had managed to bless her with two daughters who were identical in face and form and exact opposites in nature and attitude. She thought that he must have been feeling extremely creative on the day he drew up the blueprints on the two girls.

"Okay," she said, as she turned the key and the engine sprang to life. "A mile and stay to the left. We can't miss it."

The cowboy had been true to his word. The fork in the road was just over a mile. They followed the winding, dusty road for nearly another two miles before they passed under a wooden arch with "Four Aces Ranch" burned into it. Another mile passed before the ranch actually came into view, and Kathleen could breathe a sigh of relief. She barely had the van stopped before the girls were climbing out.

"Oh, this is great!" Holly declared as she turned in a slow circle, openly marveling at the unfamiliar world around her. "This is better than the Sears Tower and O'Hare put together."

Heather crossed her arms over her chest and glared at her sister, refusing to be impressed in any way whatsoever. "Give me Chicago any time."

"We're off and running," Kathleen muttered as she slipped out of the van.

"Katie!"

Kathleen looked up, the sound of her shortened name echoing through the still air. She caught a flash of blue jeans and a red work shirt before two strong arms caught her close and swung her in a wide circle. To save herself, she clung to solid shoulders until the wild ride was over and her feet were planted firmly on the ground again. She looked up into her brother's laughing face.

"I was starting to get worried," Jon Graham said. "Did you have trouble finding us?"

"Not much."

"Good." He was grinning as he turned toward the twins. "Let me get a good look at these girls."

Kathleen watched as he hugged Heather and Holly in turn and commented on how much they'd changed. The fact was, the girls had only been four when he'd last seen them. Ten years was a long time. Change was inevitable.

He hadn't changed so much, Kathleen decided. His dark hair showed some gray at the temples and the lines around his eyes were a little deeper, but for the most part he looked just as she remembered. His face and hands were deeply tanned, attesting to the fact that he spent a lot of time outside. His lean frame indicated a physical lifestyle. It was obvious that Montana agreed with him in a way Chicago never had.

He turned back to her. "Let's get you guys unloaded," he said. "Then I'll round up that wife of mine and see about supper."

Kathleen had never met Jon's wife, Mattie. They'd married three years ago, and Kathleen had been unable to attend the wedding. She was a little surprised by her sister-in-law's age, judging her to be at least ten years younger than Jon. But it was plain to see that the couple was crazy about each other. For that, Kathleen was grateful. With her emotions still raw from her own divorce, she was glad to see her brother happy in his marriage.

Mattie pushed through the swinging door dividing the kitchen and dining room and surveyed the long mahogany table through chocolate brown eyes. "Is there anything you want that I haven't thought of?"

Kathleen looked at the food laden table and couldn't imagine anything missing. "After three days of fast food restaurants, this looks wonderful."

Mattie shot her a bright smile. "Thanks." She pulled out a chair to the left of her husband's and sat down. "We might as well go ahead and start. Cody will be along in a bit."

"Did you see him?" Jon asked from his place at the head of the table.

"He just rode into the stables. He'll be a few minutes."

Jon nodded and looked around the table. "I'll offer grace," he said simply, then proceeded to do so.

A few moments later, Kathleen was biting into some of the best food she'd ever tasted. Her stomach, after days of greasy hamburgers, was eternally grateful.

"This is really good," Holly complimented as she finished off a fluffy yeast roll. "Uncle Jon said you're the main cook around here. Do you cook for the whole ranch?"

Mattie shook her head, her dark ponytail dancing. "I split the duties with a man named Lonny Jones. Between the two of us and ten full and part-time employees, we manage to keep everybody fed."

The door to the kitchen swung inward, and Kathleen looked up and into the purest green eyes she'd ever seen. She realized in the next instant that the man staring back at her was the same one they'd encountered on the road. His hat was gone, revealing dark blond hair that was far too long for the conventional standards she was used to. The features of his face were classically handsome at first glance, though there was a hardness there that made her wonder if tenderness was a foreign emotion for him.

He wore a plain cotton work shirt, the sleeves rolled back to reveal hands and forearms as tan as his face. Faded, lived-in jeans clung to his hips and thighs like second skin, giving the impression that there wasn't an ounce of extra fat on his body.

When her gaze wandered back to his face, she was startled to find his attention still focused on her. One dark brow arched slightly, and she felt her cheeks heat. Instantly, she looked away. She actually had to fight the urge to crawl under the table and hide. She'd been gawking at the man like a lovelorn adolescent and he'd caught her at it.

She'd lost all track of the conversation around her until Jon said, "Cody, let me introduce you to my sister and nieces."

Kathleen had no choice but to meet his gaze as introductions were made. He'd moved around to the opposite end of the table, well away from her, but the knowledge in those green eyes had her flushing again.

"Nice to meet you, Mr. Washington," she murmured politely.

"Call me Cody. Please."

She nodded slightly and turned her attention back to her food.

"You're the guy we saw earlier, aren't you," Heather spoke up.

"I'm the guy."

"What do you do on the ranch, Cody?" Holly asked as she handed him the bowl of green beans.

He spooned the vegetable onto his plate and then set the bowl aside. "Whatever needs to be done. Jon keeps me busy."

Holly smiled sweetly and passed him another dish. "So Uncle Jon is your boss?"

"He tries." He shot Holly a slight smile, the hard lines of his face softening. "But I'm bigger and meaner, so he never gets away with it."

Kathleen saw the effect that brief curving of his mouth had on her daughter. Actually, it had the same effect on her without even being directed her way. In addition to good looks, Cody Washington also possessed a basic sex appeal. Of course, it wasn't anything she needed to worry about. She was not the kind of woman that attracted a man's attention. Gary, her ex-husband, had made it perfectly clear that she was a disappointment in every category that mattered to a man.

"Why don't you sound like a cowboy?"

Heather's question interrupted her moody thoughts. She watched as Cody turned his attention to the girl. "Why don't you look exactly like your twin?" he challenged smoothly.

Heather's blue eyes narrowed. "Because I wanted to establish my own identity."

He studied her thoughtfully as he finished off a slice of roast beef. "Did it work?"

"Yeah. Now people don't get us confused all the time."

He looked from Heather to Holly and then back again. "So cutting all your hair off and dying it . . ." He paused and squinted his eyes a moment as if trying to determine exactly what color her hair was, ". . . that color, did the trick?"

"Yes," she said coolly. "I said it did."

He nodded slowly and shrugged. "It doesn't change anything, you know."

"What do you mean?"

"Well, you're still a blond under whatever color you've used, and your face is still the same as your sister's. Basically, nothing has changed."

Holly laughed lightly. "That's exactly what Mom told her."

Kathleen felt Cody's stare before she met it directly. Again, his mouth quirked slightly. "Smart mom," he murmured.

Why did she feel like she'd just received praise of the highest order? Her gut reactions to this man were ridiculous and dangerous. If she wasn't careful, she was going to end up making a bigger fool of herself than she already had. And that was the last thing her bruised ego needed right now.

"Well, I don't care what any of you think," Heather stated firmly. "I like my hair this way." She pinned Cody with sharp, blue eyes. "You never did answer my question. Why don't you sound like a cowboy?"

He finished off his meal and pushed his plate aside. "What do you perceive a cowboy to sound like?"

"Well, slow and with a drawl. You know, with words like 'ma'am' and 'howdy.' You know what I mean."

"Yeah, I know what you mean. When you meet some of the wranglers and cowboys on the ranch, then you'll hear what you think you should be hearing."

"Okay. But why don't I hear it from you?" she persisted. "I mean, Uncle Jon looks like a cowboy, but he doesn't sound like one because he's from Chicago. Why don't you sound like one?"

"Because I'm from Montana."

"But. . . ."

"You like to argue, don't you, Heather," he interrupted.

"It's what she does best," Holly commented smugly.

Heather shot her sister a scathing look. "Better than being all meek and docile like you."

"Okay," Kathleen intervened. "I'm not up to this, and I'm sure the rest of the people in this room don't want to hear it either."

"Why don't you girls help me with dessert?" Mattie suggested as she pushed her chair back and stood. Without comment, the two girls followed her to the kitchen.

Jon slid his sister an amused glance. "You have your hands full," he said, as the door closed behind them.

Kathleen smiled slightly. "I knew when I was carrying them that I had my hands full." She reached up to rub her forehead. "They are as different as night and day. It gets to be pretty gamey sometimes. They'll probably drive you nuts before we leave."

"You're welcome to stay as long as you want, Katie," he said gently. "You know that."

She looked down at her hands. "I know. But I can't hide out here forever. I've got to pull things together and get on with my life." She lifted her gaze to find Cody watching her with those clear green eyes. Embarrassed, she looked away. She didn't have to be a mind reader to know what his thoughts were. Sometimes when she looked in the mirror she didn't even recognize the frail, lifeless woman who stared back.

Heather stuck her head around the door. "Everybody want apple pie and ice cream?"

"Nothing for me." Cody pushed his chair back and stood. "I've got some things to see to at home." He came around the table and paused beside Jon's chair. "I'll be over early in the morning to start on that new cabin."

Jon nodded. "I'll be ready."

With a general "See you later," Cody disappeared into the kitchen.

Kathleen wondered at the vague disappointment she felt at his departure.

Dawn came quickly on the heels of a nearly sleepless night. Kathleen dressed in jeans and a black sweatshirt and went downstairs to the kitchen to find the coffee fresh and hot. She poured a cup and stepped out onto the wrap-around porch to lean against the railing. The mountain air had a chill to it, but the sun rising in a cloudless sky would soon chase it away.

Work was well underway as wranglers saddled horses for waiting guests. There was plenty of activity, but it lacked any real urgency. Everything seemed to be done with a laid-back and relaxed attitude. The scent of frying bacon drifted on a light breeze attesting to the fact that breakfast was being served. Kathleen figured if she could find the dining hall, she'd probably find Mattie, too.

She finished her coffee and set the cup on the edge of the porch, deciding she might as well try to find her way around. The sound of an approaching vehicle caught her attention, and she looked up as a dark blue pickup came into view. As she watched, the truck pulled in next to her van and the engine silenced.

Cody climbed out of the truck, surprised to see Kathleen up so early. He figured she'd be used to sleeping well into the morning. But she stood there on the steps, dressed in loose fitting jeans and a black sweatshirt that nearly swallowed her up. He had no idea what kind of body the baggy clothes concealed, but he figured a stiff breeze would probably blow her away.

"Good morning," he greeted as he strode toward her.

"Good morning."

He stopped in front of her and nearly swore out loud. The woman looked as fragile as hand-spun glass. The morning light was not kind as it stole the color from her face. Dark smudges under her eyes gave the impression that another six hours of sleep would have done her a world of good. Her eyes, a cross between a blue and a gray, were dark and full of shadows. He saw the uncertainty there, the doubts and fears, before she averted her gaze. With a nervous gesture, she reached up to tuck a stray strand of honey-blond hair behind her ear.

Cody looked at her and reminded himself that Kathleen Hunter would have to find her own way in this big, bad world. There were no magic solutions for broken hearts or broken marriages, and he didn't have any experience with either malady. He couldn't solve her problems, even if he'd wanted to.

"Have you seen Jon this morning?" He heard the edge of impatience in his voice and instantly regretted it.

She shook her head, but didn't look up. "No."

"Probably the stables or the dining hall," he decided as he studied her a moment longer. What had happened to the woman who had boldly taken his inventory when they'd met yesterday? He pushed the thought aside and asked abruptly, "Have you eaten yet?"

"No. I was on my way to the dining hall." She hesitated before casting him a cautious glance. "Could you tell me where it is?"

Inwardly he sighed. He supposed he could spend a few minutes helping her get acclimated. "Come on. I'll give you a quick tour of the place so you can find your way around."

"That's not necessary. I don't want to keep you from your work."

"Don't worry about my work. It's not going anywhere." He saw indecision tugging at her and held his hand out toward her. "Come on," he coaxed. "It'll only take a few minutes."

She looked at him and then at his hand. Finally, she came down off the porch, ignoring his gesture. He dropped his arm back to his side, and she fell into step beside him as he led the way along the gravel drive into a thickly wooded area. A light breeze rippled through the trees, rustling the branches and bringing with it the scent of pine and fresh mountain air.

Cody wasn't sure why he was so acutely aware of the woman beside him. The top of her head barely came to his shoulders, and he found himself adjusting his normally long stride to match hers. Without even trying, she punched buttons in him that brought to the forefront all kinds of protective urges. Urges that were definitely rusty from disuse over the years. Life in Montana did not produce vulnerable women. The women Cody was used to dealing with knew how to take care of themselves. They did not want or need a man to take care of them. From what little Jon had told him, Cody suspected that Kathleen had been taken care of her whole life. It was his personal opinion that she should turn around and head back to Chicago to find another man to take care of her the rest of her life.

They came to a point where the road forked. "We'll go this way," Cody said, turning toward the right. "It's a circular drive, and we'll end up at the dining hall. The cabins are down this way."

"How many are there?"

"We have twelve right now and plans to add two more for next year. They're all different sizes. Some can accommodate up to eight people." He pointed past her to the left. "Right through those trees you can see one of the larger ones."

She turned to survey the rustic structure tucked snugly within a stand of trees. "It's pretty secluded."

"They all are. That's the main reason people come up here. The solitude. They want to get away from the rat race. There's no television in the rooms and no telephone, although both are available in the recreation hall."

Silence stretched between them again as they continued to walk. Sunlight filtered through tall tree branches, leaving patchwork designs on the ground before them. Squirrels and chipmunks scurried about the tree trunks as birds called out from above. Even after living his whole life here, the unique beauty of an early Montana morning never ceased to move him. He'd traveled all over the world and had never come close to finding the tranquility this little slice of heaven offered.

He stopped, realizing Kathleen was no longer beside him. Impatiently, he turned. He saw that she had stopped within a beam of sunlight, her face lifted upward, her eyes closed. As a slow smile curved her lips, he stood there transfixed. It was as if in that single ray of light she'd found something essential, something vital to her mind or body. For just an instant, he saw the carefree child in the woman before him. He saw what she must have been like when her dreams had seemed possible and her tomorrows promised to be bright. And he saw the woman struggling to claim back some of those stolen dreams.

Her eyes opened and met his immediately, as if magically drawn there. For a long, silent moment he held her gaze. There was a sparkle in those eyes that had been missing earlier. They were as blue now as the morning sky, and her smile outshone the sun. The transformation left him speechless. And extremely unsettled.

As if suddenly embarrassed by her actions, a heated flush crept into her cheeks and she looked away. "I'm sorry," she said softly, pushing at a stone with the toe of her tennis shoe. "I must look pretty silly."

"No." The edge in his voice startled him and must have caught her attention because she looked up curiously. He met her gaze squarely. "Don't ever apologize for enjoying life, Kathleen."

He had no name for the emotion that filtered through her eyes. But a small smile appeared before she said, "Okay, I won't."

He drew in a deep breath and looked away from her. Some mysterious force was drawing him into something he knew for a fact he didn't want any part of. It became vitally important that this encounter come to an end.

"Come on," he urged, turning away from her. "The dining hall is just up ahead."

Two

Kathleen closed the book and tossed it onto the pastel colored quilt covering her bed. It was useless to try to read. She'd started the chapter twice and still didn't have a clue as to what was happening. Just like her life, she thought ruefully.

Pushing to her feet, she walked to the window and looked out into the black night. It was nearly midnight, but she was so restless she could barely stand it. Maybe some fresh air would help. She picked up her jacket from the back of the wicker rocker and shrugged into it as she slipped out of the room.

Silently she crept down the stairs, pausing at the bottom where a pool of light spilled out from Jon's office. He was working at a computer and must have sensed her presence, because he looked up just as she started past the door.

"Katie, are you okay?"

She stepped into the doorway. "I thought I'd go out on the porch for a while. I can't sleep."

He studied her thoughtfully. "It's pretty chilly out there," he cautioned.

"I won't be long."

Still he continued to watch her. "I could use a little fresh air, too." He reached over and pressed a series of buttons on the computer. Once the screen was clear he looked back at her. "Do you mind if I join you?"

"No, of course not."

"Good." He stood and came around the desk toward her. He reached behind the door and lifted his denim jacket from a hook there. When they stepped out onto the porch, the night air wrapped around them with chilly fingers. Kathleen drew in a deep breath.

"So how do you like it here after a week?" Jon asked as he walked over to sit down on the top step.

"It's beautiful. I can see why you were drawn here."

"This is my dream," he said quietly. "Few people really get to live their dreams. I know how fortunate I am."

Kathleen walked over and sat down beside him. She looked up into a diamond studded sky that seemed to be just out of her reach. A half moon cast a dim light. "I'm really glad you're happy, Jon. I know how hard it was for you to make the decision to leave Chicago and come out here."

He gave a humorless laugh. "Do you suppose Dad ever forgave me?"

She shrugged. "I don't know. He wasn't a pleasant person to be around after you left. I couldn't talk to him about you. He wouldn't let me. After he had the stroke he never regained consciousness."

She looked over at her brother, able to see his profile clearly now that her eyes had adjusted to the dark. "I really don't know how he felt about you or anything else, for that matter."

"I can't be sorry for what I did. I was dying a slow death in Chicago. I tried to explain to him how I felt. He just never wanted to listen."

"Jon." Kathleen reached over and touched his arm, drawing his attention. "Let it go. Dad had a way of molding the people closest to him into what he wanted. We both saw him do it with Mom. The only thing she ever did without his blessing was die. You tried to be what he wanted, but it was never in you to be cooped up in a Chicago office building all day long." She waved her hand outward. "I remember you dreaming about this when we were little. You knew from the very beginning what you wanted, what you needed. Don't ever regret following your heart."

He laid his hand over hers where it still rested on his arm. "How did Dad mold you, Katie?" he asked curiously.

She looked away from him, out into the darkness. "He was determined that I should marry Gary," she admitted tonelessly.

Jon swore softly as his fingers tightened on hers. "I knew there was something wrong when I found out you were getting married. I just couldn't get a straight answer out of anyone, including you."

"I didn't have any straight answers. All my answers came from Dad and Gary."

"Did you ever love Gary?" he asked bluntly.

Kathleen blinked back the sudden tears and drew in a shaky breath. "I was awed by Gary at first. He was twelve years older than me and it seemed incredible that he'd be interested in me. He was handsome and sophisticated and wealthy. All the things Dad said were important. Dad told me not to worry about love, that it would come later after Gary and I were married. I waited, but it never did happen." She sighed softly and shook her head. "I realized pretty early in the marriage that all I'd done was marry a man just like my father. Dad had wanted the perfect daughter. Gary wanted the perfect wife."

"Why didn't you leave?"

"I did once," she said faintly. "It was just after our first anniversary. I went to your apartment, but you weren't home." She gave a soft laugh. "I didn't know what to do then, so I went back home. Gary never even knew I was gone."

"Why didn't you wait for me? Why didn't you come back or call me? I would have helped you."

"A couple of days later I found out I was pregnant. That changed everything for me. It wasn't just me anymore. I had to think of my baby, too." She stared out into the night, into the past. "Gary was so pleased when he found out about the baby. For a little while I thought maybe I would grow to love him. He was so thoughtful and caring at first. But that all ended when the doctor suspected I was carrying twins and ordered an ultrasound. We found out I was carrying twin girls. Gary wanted a boy. Obviously, his perfect wife had failed him."

"Oh, God!" Jon groaned. "Katie, I didn't know. I'm sorry."

She shook her head. "There was nothing you could have done. To anyone looking on, Gary appeared to be the perfect father and husband. But we were really more like his possessions. Like his car or his house or his boat. Holly picked up on this fact fairly early. She has very few illusions about the kind of man her father is. I haven't influenced her. She's drawn her own conclusions from what she's observed over the years. Heather, however, sees Gary in a very different light. As a matter of fact, she blames me for the divorce. She seems to think that if I'd been a better wife, then Gary wouldn't have gone looking for another woman."

"She told you that?"

"Not in those exact words. But she has a way of getting her point across without saying exactly what she means. It's a skill she acquired from her father."

"Katie." Jon took her hand between both of his own and squeezed it tight. "Why didn't you leave him years ago?"

"I couldn't take that risk because I was afraid he'd use the girls as pawns. If I had been the one to file for a divorce, I know it would have been a messy affair. I didn't want to put them through that. I had planned to stay with him until they had graduated from high school."

"That's a lot of wasted years."

She turned to him, frowning. "But where would I have gone, Jon?" she whispered. "I have no skills. No way to support myself and the girls. Look at me. My divorce has been final for months, and I'm still floundering around trying to decide what to do with myself."

"You can stay here. There's plenty to be done around here. I'll just put you on the payroll and you and the girls can take one of the cabins to live in."

Kathleen shook her head. "Thank you for offering, but I can't let you do that."

"Katie. . . ."

"Listen to me," she said gently. "I'm confused about a lot of things right now, but there is one thing I know for certain. Never again am I going to depend on a man to take care of me. Don't you see that you'd be no different than Dad or Gary? You'd be just one more man looking out after helpless Kathleen."

"But I want to help you," he said roughly. "I've been damn little help when you have needed me."

She smiled. "You are helping me by letting me stay here until I decide what's best for me and the girls. You're helping me to get back on my feet. I am making progress. My being here is proof of that. I've never traveled anywhere on my own before. This trip was a challenge for me. Gary always used to laugh and say I'd get lost going to the grocery if I ever varied from my normal route. Sadly, I believed him. He tried to talk me out of making this trip, and I almost let him do it. But I suddenly realized if I'm ever going to find out who I really am, I've got to start looking for my own answers. Making this trip would not be a big deal for the normal person. But for me it was a major step toward making a new life for myself."

"I just wish I'd paid more attention to you. I wish I'd been there when you needed someone."

"You're here now when I need you," she said softly. "That's all that matters to me."

He looked at her a long moment, true regret marring his features. "I'm still worried about you," he said gently. "You've obviously lost weight, and I know you're not sleeping."

"You're right on both accounts," she admitted reluctantly. "But I figure Mattie's cooking is going to help me gain back what I need to. And I am starting to sleep better. The nights here take a little getting used to. It's a lot more quiet here than Chicago, you know."

He nodded. "I remember I had some trouble sleeping when I first came. But I know it's more than that with you. I know you've got a lot of things to work out. I want you to be happy, Katie. I know it won't be easy for you, but try to forget all the negative things Gary has drilled into your head over the years. I think you can build a new life for yourself. I think you're stronger than you think you are."

"Do you?" she murmured. Impulsively, she reached out and hugged him. "Thanks for the vote of confidence. It's the first I've had in years."

Cody cleared the top of a rocky ridge and reined Lightning to a stop. The horse danced restlessly as it caught the scent of the other horses on the road below. Cody murmured softly and ran a hand down the stallion's sleek neck. Instantly the horse calmed.

He counted sixteen riders being led by Joe Painter, the head wrangler. The set, lazy pace of the Western horses indicated that this was a group of beginner riders. He knew that Joe always took the beginners on the gravel road first before attempting one of the ranch's many riding trails.

He started to turn Lightning back when an abrupt movement at the end of the line of riders caught his attention. As he watched, one of the horses began to prance recklessly and edge closer to the ditch at the side of the road. Joe was at the front of the group and hadn't picked up on the problem in back. Someone shouted to draw his attention, further startling the nervous horse. The inexperienced rider, fighting desperately for control, was pulling hard on the reins, doing nothing more than forcing the mount to back closer to the ditch.

Cody urged Lightning down the steep incline as fast as the rocky landscape would permit. Despite the animal's sure-footed speed, they didn't arrive in time to avert disaster. They were almost to the distressed horse when it stepped off the edge of the ditch, lurched sideways, and tossed the rider from its saddle.

Cody hit the ground running and raced to where the guest lay motionless in the tall grass. Kneeling beside the still form, he reached out and snatched the cream-colored cowboy hat away, releasing a riot of honey blond curls. His breath caught in his lungs as he stared down at an unconscious Kathleen Hunter.

"Damn," he muttered.

"God, Cody, I'm sorry." Joe dropped down beside him. "By the time I realized she was in trouble, it was too late to get to her."

"Mom!" Cody heard Heather and Holly run up behind him. Carefully, he ran his hands over Kathleen's body feeling for anything that would indicate she'd broken something.

"Cody, is she okay?"

Without looking, he didn't know which of the twins issued the question. "It doesn't feel like anything is broken." He shot Joe a quick look. "Take care of the rest of the group before we lose another one."

Nodding, the other man went back to calm the other riders. Holly crouched down beside him. "I don't know what happened," she said. "The horse just started to act up all of the sudden. Mom couldn't control her."

Cody felt irritation creep in past the concern that had his heart pounding. If she would have eased her grip on the reins, the horse wouldn't have backed into the ditch. Either she hadn't been told the proper way of dealing with the animal, or she'd forgotten in her panic. He was inclined to believe the second explanation. He knew Joe was an excellent wrangler and especially careful with the novice riders.

A low moan had his gaze snapping back to Kathleen's face. As he watched, her eyes opened. She blinked a few times and lifted a hand to her forehead. Her eyes squinted as a frown creased her features. "Cody?" she murmured.

"Hello, Kathleen," he returned smoothly, giving no indication that his heart was still beating at an elevated rate.

A wry smile curved her mouth. "I think I did something wrong."

Cody sat back on his heels and lifted a hand to rub the back of his neck. Lord, the woman did strange things to him. He'd felt it the day she arrived. Her bold gaze when he'd stepped into the dining room that day had touched him like a physical caress. The walk the next morning had left him unsettled and restless. Now she was smiling that soft way she had, making him ache to reach out and pull her into his arms.

He'd done his best to avoid her the last two weeks. It didn't matter what kind of emotions she stirred in him. She didn't belong here and no doubt would be leaving soon to return to the sheltered life she was used to. Which was fine with him. He didn't like the feelings she inspired in him. He was perfectly satisfied with his life. The last thing he needed, or wanted, was a fragile, blue-eyed blond messing with his settled existence.

"Mom, are you okay?" Heather asked anxiously. "Can you move?"

Kathleen shifted gingerly and Cody leaned forward again, his hand coming to rest on her shoulder. "Take it slow," he instructed. "You might have broken something."

"I doubt it," Kathleen muttered. "Nothing other than my ego."

"Come on. I'll help you." He slipped his arm around her shoulders to brace her back.

Kathleen nearly jumped as the heat of his arm across her back seemed to flash through the cotton material of her shirt and sear her skin. He was leaning close to her, his face only inches from her own. The scent of him, strictly male and enticing, assailed her senses. Instinctively, her hand reached out and gripped his solid forearm. When she finally came to her feet, the world tipped slightly. She honestly wasn't sure if it was from the fall or from the embrace-like hold of the man beside her.

"Okay?"

His voice came low and steady close to her ear. She nodded and swallowed hard, fighting the urge to let her head drop forward to rest against his chest. "Yeah. Thanks."

He released her and climbed out of the ditch. Reaching back down, he easily lifted her out.

"Kathleen, I'm sorry," Joe apologized. "Are you sure you're okay?"

"I'm fine. It wasn't your fault," she assured him. "I was startled when Buttercup began to fidget, and I reacted by pulling too hard on the reins. I'll be okay the rest of the ride."

"You're going back to the ranch," Cody stated as he bent to pick up her hat and hand it to her.

Kathleen was struck by the stern command. She took the hat from him and lifted her eyes to meet his. "I'll be fine," she insisted. "I can go on."

"You're going back to the ranch," he said again, his green eyes steady on hers. "I'll take you."

Kathleen felt something slowly uncurl inside of her. For her entire life she'd lived with men who spoke to her with the same kind of unquestionable authority she heard now in Cody's voice. For her entire life she'd done exactly what she'd been told to do. But that life was over for her. She no longer had to do anything she didn't want to do. She was in control. She would do as she pleased.

"I'm going on," she announced, taking a step to move around him.

The feel of his fingers curling around her upper arm had her gaze flying back to his. Anger turned his eyes to hard, glittering stones. The solid set of his jaw and mouth were intimidating.

"Listen to me." Despite the silky softness of his voice there was no denying the underlying command. "It's ranch policy that if there's a riding accident, the guest returns to the ranch. You took a nasty fall. You were unconscious. Joe doesn't need for you to realize the extent of your injuries when he's miles from the ranch and medical help."

Kathleen slid a look to Joe. "Is that true?"

Joe's eyes widened slightly as he cast Cody a cautious glance. "Yes, ma'am," he said looking back at her. "It's really for your own good. Usually, I'd just return with the whole group. But since Cody's here, he can take you back and I can go on with the others."

Well, so much for taking a stand, Kathleen thought ruefully. She turned to the girls. "You two go on with the group. I'll be okay."

"Are you sure?" Holly asked.

"I'm sure. Go on now. We've held everybody up long enough."

As the girls went back to their horses Kathleen turned to Joe. "Will you keep an eye on them, please?"

He tipped his hat and smiled. "Sure thing."

"Thanks," she said, as he reined his horse around and trotted off. She watched as he once again organized everybody and they started off along the road. A few of the riders lifted their hands, and Kathleen waved back.

Her attention eventually wandered to Cody as he crossed the road and caught the reins of the two horses grazing there. She didn't have to know him well to know he was doing an admirable job of holding onto his temper.

"Let's go," he ordered as he approached her, the horses in tow.

She reached for the reins to her mount, but he held them away from her. "You're not riding the horse back."

Her brow arched in surprise. "You're going to make me walk?"

Raw fury flashed in the look he shot her. "No. You're riding with me."

"You've got to be kidding!" She gave a disbelieving laugh and eyed the huge black horse. "No way, Cody."

He finished tying the reins of her horse to his saddle horn before turning to her. "Will you just do what I say and quit arguing."

"No," she returned promptly, her own temper kicking into gear. "There is no reason why I can't ride Buttercup."

"There is if I say there is."

"Who put you in charge?" she demanded. "Why don't you just ride back to where you came from?"

"Well, excuse me for checking to see if you managed to break your foolish neck."

"You didn't have to. I'm sure Joe could have taken care of things." She spread her arms wide. "I'm not hurt, so I don't understand what the big deal is."

"I don't have time for this," he muttered just before he swung himself up into the saddle. He reached a hand down to her. "Come on."

She crossed her arms over her chest and glared up at him. "I'm not riding with you," she stated succinctly.

"Then you'll have to walk because you're not getting back on your horse."

"That's ridiculous!" she shouted. "I can ride my own horse."

"She threw you once, Kathleen. I'm not taking a chance with her again."

Kathleen blew out a frustrated breath. "Buttercup didn't throw me. I caused her to step into the ditch. It was my fault."

"Damn right it was. You're lucky she didn't break her leg, leaving Jon with one less mount."

"I'm sorry," Kathleen said, meaning it. "I panicked. I didn't mean to put the horse in any danger."

Cody shook his head and looked away from her. "Let's just go back to the ranch. It's a short ride. Surely, you can stand my presence for a few short minutes."

Kathleen stood and considered her situation. She really didn't want to walk back to the ranch, but somehow she thought Cody would let her if she declined his offer of a ride. She also didn't want to share that narrow saddle with him. Being that close to him seemed like the most dangerous solution to the problem, even if it was for a short ride.

"Dammit, Kathleen," he snapped. "I don't have the time for this."

Before she could respond, he had edged Lightning closer. She had time for one startled squeal before he leaned down and scooped her up with one strong arm around her waist. His arm stayed around her, and she found herself pressed close to the hard lines of his body. Abruptly, she jerked away from him, coming precariously close to sliding out of the saddle.

"Settle down," he warned, his breath stirring her hair. "You spook these horses and we'll both have to walk back to the ranch." He shifted and settled himself more comfortably in the saddle. "Get yourself situated," he instructed curtly.

Kathleen tried to scoot as far away from him as possible. But with the pommel in front and his rock solid thighs behind her, there was very little space to maneuver in. Finally she gave up trying. "Just go," she ordered.

His arms came around on either side of her, and she stiffened in an effort to keep from touching him. It was a losing battle. Soon her back and shoulders began to ache from the effort, forcing her to relax her ramrod straight posture. By the time they'd traveled a mile she had come to appreciate the solid strength of his chest behind her. She tried to ignore the fact that her thighs were nestled intimately to his. Instead she chose to concentrate on his hands as he easily handled the reins. His fingers were long and she suspected the palms would be rough due to the work he did. But in contrast, they were gentle in the way they handled the horse. She wondered if he handled his women with the same care.

That thought had her jerking away from him. Her wandering thoughts had obviously taken a wrong turn. It didn't matter how he was with women. She certainly didn't ever care to know. And he certainly would never be inclined to show her.

Cody couldn't remember a time he'd been more relieved to see his destination come into view. It was all he could do not to send Lightning into a wild gallop. The bottom line was he had to get Kathleen off this horse before he embarrassed himself. It had been torture enough when he'd brought her up onto the saddle and she'd wriggled around trying to get comfortable. Then he'd had to endure the scent of her drifting up to him. She smelled of sunshine and flowers and basic woman, a combination guaranteed to drive a man to distraction. And her hair, dammit. It kept blowing back against his cheek and neck like a soft caress. Why hadn't she left her hat on, or better yet, tied the silky strands back?

He'd finally taken to reciting multiplication tables just to get his mind off of her. The ploy had worked until she'd relaxed, allowing her body to rest back against his chest. Desire had flooded him then, and it was all he could do to keep his body's natural response from shocking them both.

And he was shocked. Hell, he was astounded. He felt like a damned teenager. It had certainly been that long since he'd responded to a woman like he did Kathleen. Without even trying, she'd stripped him of all control. He shuddered to think what his reaction would be if she ever set out to seduce him.

He pushed that thought away immediately. He couldn't afford to think about it right now. It didn't matter anyway. His association with Kathleen Hunter was about to come to a definite end.

Earl Shepherd stepped out of the stable and ambled forward as Cody reined Lightning to a stop. He peered up at the pair with curious brown eyes. "What happened?"

"The horse threw Kathleen," Cody returned shortly.

Earl walked up and patted Buttercup on the neck. "Now why did you go and do that, old girl?" he asked as if he expected the horse to answer.

"It was my fault," Kathleen offered. "I backed her into a ditch."

Earl arched a gray eyebrow. "Well, now, Miss Kathleen, that's not a real smart thing to do," he drawled as he hooked his thumbs under the suspenders of his overalls. "I know we taught you better than that."

Kathleen liked the old man who was in charge of overseeing all of the horses. He was a spry old fellow, probably somewhere in his sixties and about as mischievous as any six year old.

She grinned down at him. "Well, now, Earl, I reckon you're right," she returned with an imitation of his slow drawl.

"Earl, would you like to help Kathleen down?" Cody asked pointedly. He arched a brow when the old man merely pursed his lips and seemed to consider the situation. "Now, please," he added tensely.

Chuckling softly, Earl came around and guided Kathleen safely to the ground. The teasing look he sent Cody was almost enough to send a flush of color into the younger man's cheeks. Cody ignored the knowing dark eyes and concentrated on untying Buttercup's reins. Once free, he handed them to the old man.

"Find another horse for Kathleen," he ordered as he settled more comfortably into the saddle. A sudden, unbidden flash of slender hips and thighs pressed close to him had him shifting again.

"Well, now, Cody, Buttercup and Kathleen have been gettin' on together just fine all week. Maybe it was just a bad moment for both of them."

"I told you, it was my fault," Kathleen repeated. "There's nothing wrong with the horse."

"I don't want you back on that horse." Cody's voice rose with each word.

"I don't care what you want!" she shouted back. "I like the horse and I'm going to continue to ride her." She whirled to face Earl. "Do you understand me?"

"Oh, yes, ma'am," he assured her quickly.

"I don't give a damn what you want," Cody ground out. "You're playing out of your league, Kathleen. Why don't you leave the ranch decisions up to those who know what they're doing." He shot Earl a quelling look. "Find her another mount," he snapped. "Do you understand me?"

"I hear you, Cody," the old man answered calmly.

Cody swore softly. Earl may have heard him, but he sure as hell wasn't promising to do as he'd been instructed. Deciding it was all a losing battle, he turned back to Kathleen. "If I catch you on that horse," he began in a low, smooth tone, "I will personally remove you. Do you understand?"

She glared at him mutely. For a long moment he held her gaze, letting his warning hang between them. Then, abruptly, he wheeled Lightning around and galloped away.

Kathleen watched, drawn by the rough beauty of the man and horse. She didn't care what Cody said. She liked Buttercup and she would continue to ride her. Kathleen felt a sudden flash of satisfaction. She'd actually stood her ground with Cody. Despite his domineering attitude, she hadn't backed down. She couldn't deny that her new-found assertiveness felt wonderful.

Earl whistled softly and said, "I'd say Cody's just a bit upset."

"Yeah." Kathleen turned to him. "I still want to ride Buttercup. I don't care what he says."

Earl nodded. "No problem with that. I'll have her ready any time you want her."

"Thanks." She hesitated a moment. "You won't get into any trouble with Cody or Jon over this will you?"

"Nah. Don't you worry about it, Miss Kathleen." He gathered the reins and started to lead Buttercup toward the stable.

"Earl, what's Cody's position here on the ranch?" Kathleen asked.

The old man shook his head. "Cody doesn't have any position on the ranch that I know of."

Her eyes widened. "Then why is he always issuing orders to everyone?"

"Because he's good at it, I guess."

She frowned, more confused than ever. "Why does everyone jump to do whatever he says?"

"Because he's usually right." Earl reached up to rub the side of his gray whiskers. "Usually," he added, his eyes thoughtful.

With a shake of his head he turned and led the horse away, leaving Kathleen with the impossible task of making sense out of his words.

Three

The crowd at Dillon's was the usual Saturday night collection. The band on stage was loud, the liquor was good and the ladies were friendly. Cody had decided sometime after leaving Kathleen at the Four Aces Ranch three days ago that he definitely was in need of a friendly lady. So he'd come searching at the only place in Wolfe Creek where he could be assured of finding one.

Dillon's Honky Tonk sat on the outskirts of town, a ramshackle building that depended more on its widespread reputation than it did on its charming decor. Actually, it possessed very little charm. It was basically four rough wooden walls and a roof featuring a well-stocked bar, a stage for a live band, a large dance floor and plenty of seating. There was nothing trendy about the place, and Jim Dillon saw no reason to fix what wasn't broken. If folks wanted a more refined atmosphere, then they could travel the forty miles to Bozeman to get it.

Cody didn't frequent the establishment regularly, but when he did, he never had any trouble finding someone to share his evening with. He'd lived his whole life in Wolfe Creek and knew just about everybody in the small town.

Tonight he'd found himself at a table with Adam Harrison, Wolfe Creek's own professional rodeo star. Cody and Adam had gone to school together, but had never come close to being good friends. There'd always seemed to be a subtle rivalry between the two that Cody had never been able to exactly pinpoint. It was as if the two of them had been designed to purposely rub each other the wrong way. Even now after years of going their separate ways, Cody still felt the rub. And despite the fact that Adam had invited him to join his cozy little group, Cody knew that the other man felt it too.

Cody hadn't accepted the invitation because he felt the need to butt heads with Adam Harrison. He'd accepted because the little red head sitting across from Adam looked just like what Cody was in need of.

Her name was Tiffany and she was from Dallas. She loved the rodeo and had met Adam a year ago in Omaha. Since she had some vacation time to dispose of, she'd grabbed a couple of her friends and they'd come to spend a few days with Adam. Tomorrow they were all leaving to watch the bronc rider compete in Billings. Tonight they were just looking for a little fun and relaxation. Which was precisely what Cody was looking for.

Two drinks later he found himself on the smokey dance floor, a slow ballad thumping in the background and a very warm Tiffany in his arms. The curves that filled her tight jeans and western style shirt were generous and inviting. She was tall and fit nicely against him. When she drew his head downward about halfway through the song, he discovered that her mouth echoed the same promise he'd seen in her eyes. By the time the song ended he was certain he'd found what he'd come looking for.

He was having just one tiny problem. For some unknown and unfathomable reason, Kathleen's image kept floating across his mind. He kept seeing tawny hair instead of red and blue-gray eyes instead of green. And the curves that had been pressed so close to him earlier in the week had been slighter than the ones he'd just run his hands over. It infuriated him that a vulnerable woman with a soft smile would haunt him while he held a vital and willing woman in his arms. It made absolutely no sense.

Back at the table another round of drinks had been ordered and were waiting. In an effort to push Kathleen out of his mind for good, Cody scooted his chair closer to Tiffany's and draped his arm across her shoulders. She sent him a sultry smile that should have started his blood boiling. It didn't. He seriously began to doubt his sanity.

He took a long pull on his drink and listened with half an ear while Adam told a rodeo story. It wasn't until the other man stopped dead in the middle of a sentence that Cody turned his full attention to him.

"Mercy," Adam breathed, his dark eyes locked on something across the room. "I've been away too long. Who's the angel that just walked in, Cody?"

Frowning, Cody turned to look over his shoulder and nearly fell out of his chair. Kathleen stood just inside the door looking a little tentative, but more beautiful than he ever would have imagined. He'd never seen her in anything but loose jeans and baggy shirts. Now he saw exactly what he'd been missing.

Her denim skirt was snug, giving special emphasis to the soft swell of her hips. The hem struck her just above the knees, exposing shapely legs. Her long sleeve blouse was a vivid cobalt blue and tucked into the waist of her skirt. There was really nothing sexy about it unless you counted the way it tantalized the eye by dipping into a suggestive vee between her breasts

At least it appeared suggestive to Cody. What in the hell was she doing here? The last place she needed to be was alone in a bar with a bunch of fun-loving cowboys. If he had to be the one to point that out to her, then so be it.

He started to stand just as Jon and Mattie came in the door behind her. Dropping back into his chair, Cody turned and reached for his drink, finishing it in one long swallow.

Adam pushed his chair back and stood. He shot a sharp look at Cody. "Is she related to Jon or Mattie?"

"Jon's sister," came the terse reply.

Adam grinned and smacked his hand on the table. "Thanks," he said before heading across the room.

Cody leaned forward and rested his elbows on the table while he ran his hands over his face. It was almost laughable. Adam was very much a wolf on the prowl and Kathleen was as innocent as a newborn lamb. God, how had this night gone so wrong?

"Are you okay, Cody?" Long fingers ran a trail up and down his back. Tiffany. He'd forgotten about her. When he'd entered the bar earlier, he'd decided that she was the one to ease the tension in him. But he admitted now that he'd only been kidding himself. What he was really looking for was not going to be found in her generous arms.

"Hi, Cody. What a surprise to see you here tonight."

He looked up at Mattie's greeting and smiled slightly. "I could say the same about you."

"We thought we'd show Katie some of the local night life," Jon said.

"Actually, it's the only night life Wolfe Creek has to offer," Adam explained. "But it's really pretty good for a small town. You guys will join us, won't you?"

Jon shrugged. "Sure."

Chairs were pulled over from other tables as Adam made introductions. When everyone was finally seated, Cody wasn't the least bit surprised to find Kathleen occupying the chair next to Adam and across from him. He had refrained from looking at her, but it was damned near impossible when she was directly in his line of vision. The gold hoops dangling from her ears kept catching the light and drawing his attention. And what had she done to her hair? It was tossed about her head in a careless style that had his fingers itching to glide through the strands. There was nothing vulnerable about this woman who seemed to be enthralled with Adam Harrison. She appeared quite capable of being able to take care of herself.

Abruptly, Cody pushed to his feet and reached for Tiffany's hand. "Let's dance," he suggested shortly.

He soon discovered, however, that the dance floor wasn't far enough. His gaze kept drifting to the table. Jon and Mattie had decided to dance, also, leaving Kathleen alone with Adam. His arm was stretched along the back of her chair, and her head was tilted toward him as she seemed to listen intently to what he was saying.

They made a striking couple with his dark good looks and her fragile beauty. Cody had the urge to kick something.

"Would you like to leave?" Tiffany suggested as she nuzzled his neck. "We can go back to my room."

Now there was an idea. All he had to do was turn and walk out the door with this incredibly sensual woman on his arm. He would bet almost anything he owned that after a few minutes in her arms, he would forget all about Kathleen Hunter. At least until the sexual rush was over.

He stopped dancing and looked down at her. He didn't understand this obsession with Kathleen that had claimed him, but until he did, he knew he wouldn't be going anywhere with Tiffany or any other woman.

"I'm sorry," he said softly, bringing his hands up to her shoulders. "You're a beautiful lady, but I don't think going back to your room is such a good idea for me."

A knowing smile curved her lips. "I thought you might say that." She looped her arms loosely around his neck. "I think we started out on the same track, but you got derailed somewhere along the way."

He gave a quiet laugh. "That's one way of putting it."

"Too bad." Her sigh was regretful. "It could have been quite a night."

"I don't doubt it," he murmured. He felt her fingers tighten at the back of his head drawing him downward. It was a kiss designed strictly to reel a man in and land him. Cody could remember being persuaded by less. But on this particular night it set off little more than a pleasant ripple.

Tiffany finally drew away and looked up at him. She shrugged lightly and smiled. "You can't blame a girl for trying."

"Come on," he said, guiding her back toward the table. "I'll buy you another drink."

"Go ahead and order," she said. "I need to make a stop in the ladies' room."

He made his way back to the table and found it empty except for Jon. "Where's Mattie?" he asked, sliding into his chair.

Jon pointed toward the crowded dance floor. "Out there with Joe. I told her she could dance all those fast ones with the other guys. But I'm the only one she dances the slow ones with."

Cody grinned. "Sounds smart to me."

His gaze wandered the dance floor. He told himself he wasn't looking for Kathleen, but when he finally located her, he didn't shift his attention. Adam was trying to teach her some fancy dance step. She gave it a try, got her feet all tangled up and collapsed against him overcome with laughter. The man's arms came up to wrap around her, and Cody had to force himself to stay in his chair.

"What are you scowling about?" Jon asked.

"Nothing," Cody answered sharply. The waitress returned with the drinks he'd ordered. He tossed back half of his in one swallow.

Jon arched a brow and turned thoughtful eyes to the dance floor. "Katie sure does seem to be enjoying herself," he said easily.

"Kathleen better watch the message she's putting out or she's going to find herself with more trouble than she can handle," Cody predicted harshly.

Jon reached up and ran a hand over his jaw. "I don't know. She is thirty-four. Surely she's figured out by now how much she can handle."

"The men are a little different out here. They're not the refined gentlemen she's used to."

Jon turned dark eyes to his friend. "You include yourself in that assessment, Cody?"

Cody drained his glass and set it down with a loud thump. "Especially myself." He pushed his chair back and stood.

The music had changed to a slow number and the dancers were shifting on the dance floor. When it became obvious that Adam and Kathleen weren't going to sit this one out, Cody made his way through the crowd.

Kathleen couldn't remember the last time she'd had so much fun. It had to have been at least fifteen years because she was sure she'd never felt this way with Gary. She was relaxed, as if she didn't have a care in the world. It must be Adam's influence, she decided. He was so laid back and easy to be with. She looked up into his handsome face. He smiled the kind of smile that lit his eyes and made her feel like a very desirable woman. A warm glow of satisfaction washed over her. All of her life she'd always felt inadequate, both emotionally and physically. But something in Adam's eyes made her feel that all the pieces were there and in the right places.

"Mind if I cut in?"

Kathleen looked up and felt a little of her contentment evaporate. She'd already pegged Cody Washington in the same category as her father and Gary: a dominant man who always had to be in control.

"Come on, Cody," Adam cajoled. "Katie and I are just getting to know one another."

"I can see that," Cody returned pointedly. "Be a gentleman, Adam. I know it's a stretch, but give it a try."

Kathleen felt Adam stiffen at the insult. She sighed and sent Cody an annoyed look. "It's okay, Adam," she said, smiling up at him. "Why don't you go back to the table and order me another of whatever I've been drinking."

He hesitated, but finally relinquished his place to Cody. He cast Cody one brief look that spoke volumes before turning to leave the floor.

"How many of those drinks have you had?" Cody asked as he took her hand and drew her close.

She made sure a respectable distance remained between them as they began to move. "I don't know," she admitted, "but I'm sure I'm far behind you."

"No doubt," he muttered, studying her. "If your flushed cheeks and bright eyes are any indication though, I'd suggest that you slow down some."

"And we both know how good you are at suggesting."

"Well, since I'm so good at it and you're so good at listening to me, let me make another suggestion." He ignored her derisive chuckle. "Watch your step with the rodeo star. He's not as sweet and innocent as he'd have you believe."

"Is that right?" she returned mildly. "I'll take it under consideration."

He shook his head. "When monkeys fly. You're not going to listen to me and we both know it."

"Well, why should I? You're warning me off Adam, but you practically devoured that red head out here in the middle of the dance floor earlier."

He arched a brow. "Jealous, Kathleen?"

"Please!" She rolled her eyes. "You flatter yourself, Cody."

He just smiled that calm, superior smile that infuriated her. She quickly lowered her gaze. It was then that she realized that some-how, without her knowledge, he had managed to close the gap between them until there was barely any space at all. The feel of her breasts brushing lightly against his chest set off a series of erratic flutters through her system. It was strange because Adam had held her much closer and she'd felt none of the skittering sen-sations she did now. She tried to ease back, but Cody's arm was like a steel band across her back.

She lifted her gaze to his face and found him watching her with an intensity that seemed to immediately short-circuit her logical thought process. Awareness, sharp and edgy, simmered between them, and genuine alarm set her pulse to racing.

Grasping at any topic to break the tense moment, she blurted, "Why is it that you feel the need to constantly issue me orders?"

He shrugged. "I don't know," he answered honestly. "It just seems necessary with you."

She gave a humorless laugh. "Well, it's not. I've been ordered around my entire life. I've recently decided that it's time to claim my life back and live it the way I want. I don't need you, or any man, to tell me what I can or can't do."

Kathleen felt him tense and knew she'd hit her mark. When she met his gaze again, the green had definitely frosted over.

"Rest assured that I have no desire to interfere in your life in any way, shape, or form," he informed her coldly. "It's my own personal opinion that the sooner you go back to Chicago the better. You don't belong here and never will. You're too soft for this kind of life."

She pushed away, breaking free of his embrace. Fury raced through her, building with an unreasonable speed and force as it went. It was practically a physical substance radiating from her body. "Don't you ever tell me what to do again," she said, her voice growing in volume with each word. "I don't give a damn about your opinions or your suggestions. I will ride whatever horse I want. I will stay in Montana if I so decide. I will dance with whomever I choose. As a matter of fact, if I want to sleep with every man in this room, I'll do that, too!"

Cheers rose up around her in response to her last assertion. She blinked, momentarily stunned by the reaction. She'd been so caught up in her anger that she'd totally lost track of where she was. Obviously, the crowd had enjoyed her impassioned speech coming at the end of the song.

A cowboy, who looked like he was easily sporting three weeks worth of trail dust, stepped up to her. "I'd like to volunteer to be first, ma'am," he said, grinning hopefully.

Kathleen stared at him, horrified at what she'd started.

"Sorry, friend," Cody snapped, stepping around the dusty cowboy. "The lady got a little carried away." His fingers clamped around her upper arm, and he started to haul her toward the door. Kathleen knew she could either try to keep up with him or be dragged along behind him. Cool night air was a welcome relief as they emerged outside. Cody didn't break his stride, and Kathleen found herself jogging to stay even with him.

When they reached his truck, he swung her around and pushed her back against the passenger door. He released her arm, but braced his hands on either side of her head and leaned his body into hers, effectively trapping her there. "If anyone is going to be first, it'll be me," he rasped seconds before his mouth swooped down to cover hers.

Immediately, Kathleen's mind closed down and pure sensation took over. There was no gentleness in his kiss. It was fierce and possessive, and she opened to him willingly. He tasted of bourbon and smokey passion. His hands had come up to tangle in her hair, holding her still while he continued to wring every last drop of response from her. He set fire to her body where his thighs cradled hers and his chest pressed against her breasts. She yearned to touch him, but her arms were caught awkwardly at her sides.

Finally, when she was sure he had taken all she had to give, he tore his mouth from hers. A low moan echoed in the stillness as he rested his forehead against her head, his fingers still moving restlessly in her hair. She could hear his harsh breathing, feel the unsteady rise and fall of his chest as he struggled for air.

Kathleen felt a multitude of conflicting emotions rush at her from every conceivable direction and knew it would take a clearer mind than she possessed at this point in time to sort it all out. Now, she concentrated mainly on pulling air into her lungs and keeping her knees solid enough to support her weight.

Cody released her and backed away. Cool air instantly filled the void, sending chills along her nerve endings. She lifted her hands to rub her arms and restore some warmth.

"Kathleen. . . ."

"I think I see his truck over there, Jon." Mattie's voice called out in the distance.

Kathleen heard Cody let out a frustrated breath, but she couldn't bring herself to look at him. She'd heard regret in his voice when he'd said her name. It would hurt too much to see it in his eyes now.

"You better go," he said quietly.

She hesitated before lifting her gaze to his. His face was partially concealed by the deep shadows surrounding them. She didn't know that he had moved until she felt his hand gently cup her cheek. He bent toward her and placed an achingly tender kiss on her lips.

"Good night, Kathleen," he whispered against her mouth.

He left her then, and she was amazed to discover herself more disoriented by his show of tenderness than she had been by his earlier forcefulness. Slowly, she turned and walked away. By the time she reached Mattie and Jon, Cody was pulling his truck out of the parking lot.

"Mom? How much longer are we going to stay here?" Heather asked.

Kathleen looked up from the chore they were sharing of wrapping silverware in paper napkins. "It's only been three weeks, honey."

"Feels like three years."

Kathleen smiled and turned her attention back to her task. "Heather, has it really been that bad or are you just determined to be miserable?"

"I am miserable," she insisted. "I miss my friends in Chicago and. . . ."

Kathleen slid her a curious glance. "And?" she prompted.

"I miss Daddy," she blurted. "Why hasn't he called since we got here? You did tell him we were coming, didn't you?"

"You know I did." Kathleen sighed, not knowing how to answer her daughter's question. In the time since their divorce had become final, Gary hadn't been particularly regular in contacting his daughters. She hadn't been surprised, but his cavalier attitude hurt the girls, especially Heather. Kathleen resented the fact that she was left with the responsibility of coming up with plausible explanations for his long stretches of silence.

Finally, she just shook her head. "I don't know why he hasn't called," she admitted. "You know how busy he gets sometimes."

The weak offering was met by a long, thoughtful silence. Kathleen could almost see the wheels turning beneath Heather's copper curls. A rueful smile touched Kathleen's mouth when she thought of Gary encountering this "new" Heather. After nearly a month, Kathleen no longer shuddered when she looked at her oldest twin. When Heather had proudly unveiled her new style, Kathleen had nearly fainted. Not only had the child hacked her long blond hair off close to the scalp, but she'd also dyed it a color somewhere between red and brown. When the girls had been little, Gary had protested any time Kathleen had dared to even trim their hair. Well, he was in for one rude shock when he next encountered his girls.

"Do you think Dad will marry Jackie?" Heather asked suddenly.

Only if she's smart enough to get pregnant, Kathleen thought spitefully. Immediately, she regretted the thought. Jackie Ward had not been the reason for the breakdown of her and Gary's relationship. That had happened years before Jackie arrived on the scene.

"I guess you'd have to ask your dad that. I couldn't say," Kathleen answered briskly. She finished the last of the silverware and carried it down to stack it in the bin at the end of the long serving line.

"Do you ever miss him?"

Kathleen's hands paused and she lifted her gaze to her daughter. Blue eyes stared back at her boldly. Kathleen heard the challenge in the question and carefully considered her response. Slowly, she moved back to where Heather stood.

"When you're older, Heather, this will all make better sense to you. What you need to understand now is that there were no winners here." She reached out and touched Heather's cheek. "There are also no enemies. Stop trying to cast me in the role of the bad guy."

Heather stared at her a long moment before her gaze dropped. She moved slightly, causing Kathleen's hand to fall away. "You've changed since we've come here," she said in a low voice.

"I've changed?" Kathleen's surprise sounded clearly in her voice. This was a new twist. "Tell me how."

Heather shrugged, her expression sullen. "You seem happier here. Like you might want to stay."

"Well, you're right, I guess. I am happier. And maybe I will want to stay."

Kathleen's error was immediately apparent. Heather's head snapped up, her eyes shining with true teenage rebellion. "I won't stay here," she announced defiantly. "You might as well know that right now. I'll call Daddy and go to live with him."

"Heather. . . ."

"No, I don't want to listen to you." She shrugged out of her work apron and slapped it down on the counter. "You're just thinking of yourself. Nothing is going to make me stay here."

Before Kathleen could move, Heather was around the counter and racing across the dining room. A moment later, the slamming of the outside door vibrated the old building.

Kathleen dropped her head and reached up to rub her eyes. Damn. Every time she thought she might be making a little progress with Heather, it turned into a fresh battle. The war had begun the night she and Gary had broken the news to the girls that a divorce was in the works. Heather's strong negative response had caught both parents off guard. But like always, Gary had left the clean-up to Kathleen. He didn't have time for emotional scenes. That was Kathleen's forte.

He didn't know it yet, but Gary had a surprise coming. In the fog of her own turmoil, Kathleen hadn't stopped to consider why he had been so generous with the divorce settlement. At first she had been naive enough to believe he actually wanted to see that she and the girls were well taken care of. Gradually, it had dawned on her that what he had actually done was appease his guilty conscience. He had paid her off, and she hadn't even been smart enough to realize it.

Well, she was through being the bad guy. Their marriage may have ended, had in fact been over for years, but he was still a father whether he wanted to be or not. This problem with Heather wasn't going to get any better until he stepped in and helped take care of it.

Kathleen didn't doubt for a minute that Heather would campaign long and hard for her return to Chicago. Kathleen also knew that Gary would never allow it. He didn't want the responsibility. He never had. And as sure as she knew how his refusal would devastate Heather, she also knew that Heather would lay the blame squarely at her feet. It would be her fault because she'd made the decision to stay in Montana.

Kathleen was in a no-win situation, but she wasn't going to stay there. It was time to give her ex-husband a call and break some new ground.

Four

The scrape of boots on the wooden floor broke into Kathleen's thoughts. Expecting one of the guests, she turned with a smile in place. At the sight of Cody, her pulse gave a startled lurch and the smile vanished.

"Nice to see you, too," he remarked wryly.

"I thought you must have fallen off a mountain or something," she returned. Nearly a full week had passed since their encounter at Dillon's. In all that time she hadn't caught even a glimpse of him. It didn't help matters that she still wasn't sure how she felt about what had happened. Her emotions seemed to run the complete gamut from outrage to yearning. Her indecisiveness only annoyed her more.

"I've been busy." He moved a few more steps into the room, and she found herself appreciating the hard lines that defined his body. He carried his hat in his hands and his unruly hair fell across his forehead with charming disarray. The man was a definite credit to the romantic illusion of the cowboy. She nearly sighed before catching herself. Lord, she was such a sucker.

Gathering up a handful of wrapped silverware, she moved to the opposite end of the counter and away from him. "Well, did you want something in particular or did you just come in here to harass me?"

"I came in to talk to you. Is that okay?"

"You want to talk to me?" Her eyes widened with mock disbelief. "Are you sure you've got the right person? I thought all you did was yell at me."

She saw his jaw tighten and felt a twinge of guilt. It appeared that he was trying to be nice. She wondered if she should run for cover. "Okay," she conceded, coming back down the counter toward him. "What do you want to talk about?"

He relaxed a little. "I thought we might go for a horseback ride. To my place." He hesitated and slapped the hat against his thigh. "My father would like to meet you."

She stared at him, truly stunned. "Your father?"

"Yeah."

He shifted and lowered his gaze. She had the oddest feeling that he was uncomfortable. What an intriguing thought. "Why?" she asked suspiciously.

Irritation flashed like lightning through his green eyes. Whether aimed at her or his father, she wasn't sure. "He says he'd like to meet the woman that I'd make a fool of myself in public with."

Kathleen's brow arched. "It's such a rare event that it calls for a personal introduction?" she chided.

"Rare?" He gave a humorless laugh. "Try non-existent. To date, I can't recall ever being involved in a shouting match with a woman in the middle of a crowded dance floor." He paused and considered her a moment. "But then I've never had a woman provoke me the way you do."

"Well, why is that?" she asked, truly wanting to know. "I've never had anyone react to me the way you have. I've never caused much of a ripple one way or the other in people." Actually, her whole life had been nearly emotionless. Gary had seldom raised his voice. He had issued all of his commands and desires in the same level, unaffected tone. No matter how justified she might have been in her anger at the time, his calm, authoritative manner had always made her feel foolish and immature. And responsible. Everything that had gone wrong had been her fault. Or so it had always seemed.

Cody settled his hat back on his head. "Let's just call it a character flaw and leave it at that," he suggested evenly. "Do you want to go with me or not?"

She hesitated and watched the impatience sizzle in his eyes. After a moment, she shrugged. "Sure. Why not."

"Thank you," he returned sardonically. He turned and started for the door. "I'll get you a horse."

"Make sure it's Buttercup."

His step faltered slightly, but he didn't stop or turn back.

* * *

Kathleen had expected Cody's house to be a quaint cabin nestled at the edge of the woods, functional and suiting the lifestyle of two men on their own. She was not prepared for the scene before her when they came over the rise of land and looked down over the sun-drenched valley below.

The first thing that caught her eye was the lawn. Lush green grass, acres of it, stretched out to the white split rail fence sketching patterns around the pastures and stables. A rich green field of alfalfa swayed gently in the breeze. Irrigation equipment sat motionless in a field of wheat that seemed to stretch to the horizon and beyond.

A paved driveway ran around the side of the house to a three car garage behind it. Colorful flowers skirted the base of the rambling blue and white clapboard house creating a riot of color. Even though it was an extravagant setting in the middle of unpretentious surroundings, it didn't look out of place. Somehow, it seemed to fit in.

Kathleen slid her gaze to Cody and found him watching her, his expression guarded. "I get the feeling there's a lot I don't know about you," she said mildly.

He pushed his hat back from his forehead. "I'd venture to say that you know close to nothing about me."

"Which is exactly how you've wanted it."

He shrugged lightly, his gaze scanning the land.

"Earl told me that you don't have a position at the Four Aces."

He looked at her then. "I never told you I worked there."

"No, but you knew I assumed you did."

He shrugged again. "If you would have asked, I would have told you."

Kathleen felt her temper begin to smolder. He had to be one of the most irritating human beings God had seen fit to put on this earth. She drew in a deep, calming breath.

"Okay, I'm asking now. What is your connection with Jon and the ranch?"

Lightning shifted restlessly and Cody tightened his hold on the reins. "Jon came here with a dream. All I've done is help him make it into reality."

She frowned. "So you gave him the money to build the ranch, or what?"

"It's a business arrangement, Kathleen. Actually, I'm only the middleman. The business is between Jon and my dad. I just brought the two of them together."

"Your dad," she said thoughtfully, peering at the valley before her. "Am I going to recognize your dad's name when I hear it?"

"That depends. If you're familiar with the art world, then you might."

"I did a lot of volunteer work at a small museum in Chicago that specializes in western art."

"Then you'll probably recognize the name."

"Olan Washington," she said softly.

"Guilty."

Well, that explained the opulence before her. Olan Washington was one of America's most gifted artists. His unique style and natural talent were readily acknowledged throughout the art world. Drawing on his love of the old west in particular and nature in general, he'd created hundreds of paintings over the years.

"My grandfather originally settled here," Cody explained. "The house he built sits just north of the main house in that stand of trees." He pointed and she followed his directions. She could just make out the form of the cabin in the shadows. "That's where I live," he continued. "It's been modernized and suits my needs just fine."

"So your father wanders around that big house all by himself?"

"More or less. My mother died almost four years ago. When she was living, she loved to entertain. It seemed there was always someone staying with us."

"This looks like a pretty big operation. Does your father have time to run it? Or do you?"

Cody shook his head. "Obviously Dad's talents lay elsewhere. My grandfather was very proud of dad's accomplishments, although this land meant everything to him. When I came along, it was soon evident that I hadn't inherited an ounce of my father's artistic abilities. But I had inherited my grandfather's love for the land. It's in my blood, just as it was his." A satisfied smile curved his mouth. "Because of dad's career I was able to travel all over the world. But there was never any doubt that everything I'd ever want or need could be found right here." He urged Lightning into motion. "Come on. I'll show you around."

A few minutes later Kathleen found herself stepping into the cool foyer of the ranch house. As expected, the style was rustic and open with lustrous hardwood floors and a scattering of Indian rugs. A staircase leading to the second floor was directly in front of her, its banister gleaming. To the left was a formal dining room. To the right, she looked through double wide doors into a room that she would define as a den. Warm cherry wood paneling covered the walls. A massive desk sat at the far end of the room, a sofa and chairs grouped comfortably across from it. The long stone fireplace directly across from the opened doors automatically dominated the room, but it was the painting centered over it that caught her attention.

"Go on in," Cody invited. "I'll go round up Dad."

Kathleen walked into the room and went straight to the painting. She stood looking up at it, intrigued by the scene it depicted. It was Montana at its best. Olan Washington was known for the authenticity he brought to his work. She knew she would recognize the view before her if she ever stumbled upon it in the real world.

Unrelenting mountains, shadowed in blues and grays, overlooked the gentle sway of an open meadow. Grazing horses and a lone female rider, her dark hair blowing in the wind, were off to the side, as if added as an afterthought. The sky was done in bold splashes of red and orange, with a blending of mauve and pink and peach. It was done at sunset, she was sure.

"Do you like it?"

Kathleen turned in response to the curious inquiry. The man standing just inside the doorway was an older version of his son. His hair was a thick silver and his face lined with age, but he moved toward her with the grace of a man years younger and physically fit.

"It's wonderful," she said. "I'd like to see where you painted it."

Regret lit his sharp green eyes as he shook his head. "I'm afraid I can't share that with you. You see, that little piece of heaven only exists here." He touched his head. "And here." He touched his chest just above his heart. "It's my own personal paradise."

With this knowledge in mind, she turned to study the painting again. He came to stand beside her. She looked over at him and smiled. "I think then that it's even more wonderful."

He returned her smile and extended his hand. "Thank you. You must be Kathleen Hunter. I'm Olan Washington."

As his fingers closed around hers she couldn't help but feel a little awed by the amount of talent possessed in that one hand. "It's a pleasure to meet you."

"Well, I hope you don't feel as if you've been summoned. But I've been quite anxious to meet the woman who's brave enough to take on my son."

Kathleen flushed. "I don't think it was bravery," she admitted ruefully. "I think it was a little too much to drink."

His deep laughter rang out as he patted the back of her hand. "I've always admired a woman who could be honest even when it wasn't to her benefit." He released her hand. "Can I get you a drink now?"

"Jenny's bringing it." Cody came into the room. "I guess you two have met."

"We have." Olan looked to his son. "We were just discussing the location of the painting."

"Ah, the elusive location. Did you share the secret with her?"

"I did."

Cody arched a brow at Kathleen. "You should feel honored. Dad isn't above fabricating fantastic stories to go with that picture and all the dangers involved in painting it." He cast his father a teasing grin that nearly knocked Kathleen off her feet. She'd never seen such a carefree expression cross his features before. If he ever aimed one of those in her direction, she was afraid she'd melt at his feet.

"There you go tarnishing my reputation," Olan admonished. "What will our guest think? Please." He motioned toward the sofa and chairs. "Have a seat, Kathleen. May I call you Kathleen?"

"Yes, of course." She sat down in a wing chair covered in a royal blue brocade.

"And you must call me Olan. None of this Mr. Washington business. It makes me feel like an old man." He sat down on the matching sofa across from her.

Kathleen laughed softly. "I wouldn't want to do that."

A young woman entered the room carrying a tray of filled glasses. Cody moved to retrieve it from her and set it on a nearby table.

"Thanks," she said, smiling up at him.

"Jenny." Olan stood. "Come meet Kathleen."

She came to Olan's side and extended her hand as he made introductions. Kathleen was struck by the other woman's classic beauty. She judged her age to be no more than twenty-five. Her skin was flawless, her eyes a clear, deep blue. Red-gold curls spilled over her shoulders and down her back nearly to her waist.

"It's a pleasure to meet you, Kathleen." Her voice hinted at a very proper eastern upbringing. "I'm glad you could come by to see us. We don't get many visitors out here, as you might imagine."

Cody passed around the iced tea as Jenny settled onto the sofa beside Olan. Though nothing had been said, Kathleen had the distinct impression that Jenny held an important position in the household. She just wasn't sure what it might be.

"So how do you like Montana?" Olan asked as he settled back against the thick cushions.

"It's beautiful. After living in Chicago all my life, I wasn't sure how I'd like it. But I'm even thinking about staying."

"Wonderful!" Olan exclaimed. "There's certainly enough room in this state for one more."

"It would be three more, wouldn't it," Jenny said. "Cody said you have twin daughters."

"Yes, I do. Heather and Holly. They're fourteen." She took a sip of her tea. "Holly is ready to move lock, stock and barrel here. Heather, however, is less than thrilled with the idea."

"Well, fourteen is a hard age in the best of circumstances," Jenny observed.

Kathleen nodded. "It's been a year of changes for all of us. Heather just hasn't adapted as well as I expected her to." She watched curiously as Cody wandered restlessly toward the windows facing the west. Nearly the entire wall was glass, granting an unobstructed view of lush rolling hillsides and mountains. It was breathtaking in its simplicity.

"Don't mind my son," Olan said, following her gaze. "He has a restless spirit. He was born a century or so too late."

"To a man who lives and breathes the old west," Jenny put in. "Actually, they were both born a century too late."

"So true." Olan sighed and set his glass aside. "What I wouldn't give to view this land before we came in and ruined it. The only people to truly appreciate or understand it were the Indians, and we stole it from them."

"Don't get started, Dad." Cody turned from the window. "I spirited Kathleen away from the dining hall. Mattie will have my hide if I don't get her back for the lunch rush."

Jenny looked across to Kathleen. "If you do decide to stay in Montana, will you live and work on the ranch?"

Kathleen shook her head. "Jon offered, but I don't think it would be a good idea. It's not that I don't like the work. There's definitely plenty there to keep me and the girls busy." She gave a self-conscious laugh. "I just feel like I need to do something on my own without a father, husband, or brother calling the shots. Unfortunately, there's not a large market for a professional mother here or anywhere else."

She felt her cheeks heat. Why in the world was she blurting all this out now? As kind as these people were, she doubted that they were interested in her messed-up life. Even with the width of the room between them, she could feel Cody's sharp gaze boring into her. What was it that caused her to continue to make a fool of herself in front of him?

"Didn't you say you worked at a museum in Chicago?" Cody asked.

"Only as a volunteer," she clarified quickly.

"Which museum was it?" Olan asked.

"The Wainright Museum of Western Art. It's not a very big place."

A slight frown creased his features as he shot a quick glance to his son. "I believe I donated two of my paintings to them," he said easily.

"Yes." Kathleen smiled, pleased that he remembered. "They were both of Custer's battlefield."

He nodded slowly, his expression thoughtful. "Yes."

"I loved those paintings from the moment I first saw them," Kathleen said, unaware that her eyes had brightened with undisguised pleasure. "I didn't fully appreciate them, though, until we stopped at Custer's battlefield on the way here. It wasn't until I actually drove through the area and walked out on those hillsides that I realized the magnitude of the event. I had always pictured the battlefield as this flat, confined area. I had no idea that it covered four and a half miles and had actually been several separate battles over a two day period. Knowing the real history makes your paintings much more emotional.

"I mean, the painting that shows Custer and his men on the open hillside with the Indians coming at them from every direction, is very dramatic. But the second one, where you show the simple white markers on that lonely hillside depicting where the soldiers fell in battle, is so moving. When I stood there on that hillside, and looked down over those markers, it was as if I could feel the spirits of all those brave men. You captured that emotion on canvas and. . . ."

She stopped in mid-sentence, her gaze flying from Olan to Jenny and finally Cody. He'd moved closer, his eyes intent as he watched her. Hot embarrassment flooded her cheeks.

"I'm sorry," she said softly, looking down at her hands. "I get carried away some times."

"Please don't apologize, Kathleen," Olan said gently.

She chanced a quick glance and found him smiling. He reached across for her hand. "There is nothing more gratifying to an artist than to hear his work described in such a passionate way. Few people truly feel the emotion that goes into a work of art. You, Kathleen, seem to be one of those lucky people."

"I am," she said, looking into his eyes and feeling some kind of basic connection. "It's as if I can step right into a painting or picture and be a part of it. I can feel it somehow."

Olan nodded, as if he understood her perfectly. "Have you ever tried creating something yourself?"

"Oh, no. I don't have any talent for that."

"Are you sure?"

"Yes, I. . . ." She stopped and stared at him. Was she sure? Once, a long time ago, she had signed up for evening art classes at the museum. She had attended two sessions before Gary insisted she drop out and spend her evenings at home with the girls. When she'd told him that she really enjoyed the classes, he'd just laughed and said that it was highly unlikely that she would be another Picasso. And if she couldn't be another Picasso, then what was the point in pursuing it?

She jumped up, suddenly so angry she was shaking. Her whole life could be condensed into one stark, unadorned paragraph. It was so lacking in detail and color that it was practically nonexistent. Where had she been the last thirty-four years? She could forgive herself the years she'd spent under her father's influence. But how could she ever justify willingly spending fifteen years with a man who robbed her of every ounce of self-esteem and pride she had? And she'd endured it with only a few weak protests. When it came down to the bottom line she was the only one to blame for her less than dazzling existence.

"I'm sorry," she said, tears thickening her voice. "I need to leave."

With her head bent, she rushed from the room.

Cody found her on the front porch. She was standing on the top step, her shoulder braced against a supporting pillar.

"I don't know where my horse is," she said without turning.

He heard the tears in her voice and felt a reaction deep in his gut. He'd never been a sucker for a woman's tears. Why he responded to this woman's tears was just another piece to a puzzle he was finding increasingly difficult to solve.

He knew he was in up to his knees and sinking fast. Each encounter with Kathleen only sucked him deeper into the mire. He couldn't explain it. It defied logical explanation. It intrigued and annoyed him. He'd tried ignoring it for the last three weeks and hadn't gained an inch. Something told him he might as well quit struggling and just go along for the ride.

He moved over to stand behind her. After a moment's hesitation, he lifted his hands and gently cupped her shoulders. He felt her tremble as she drew in a ragged breath. And then, much to his amazement, she leaned back against the wall of his chest. She felt small and fragile, and he had an overwhelming urge to wrap his arms around her to keep her safe. Instinctively, he knew that she wouldn't welcome the gesture. She wasn't looking to be wrapped in someone else's strength. She was looking to find her own.

"I let him take it all, Cody," she said, her voice shaking. "For fifteen years I let him strip me of my pride and self-esteem. I want to be angry with him, but how can I? I never tried to stop him. Or if I did, I never tried hard enough."

Cody's fingers tightened. He was having absolutely no trouble being angry with her ex-husband. As a matter of fact, if the other man had been there right now, Cody would have taken great pleasure in physically venting some of that anger. Gary Hunter was a bastard. And that was the nicest thing Cody would ever say about him.

"Don't look back, Kathleen, unless that's the way you plan to go. Keep moving forward away from the past."

She drew in a deep breath and let it out slowly. "How?" she whispered.

"The same way you've been doing it since you arrived here. You are making progress, you know." Without conscious thought, his fingers began to gently knead her shoulders. Her scent, subtle and potent, floated up to him. Desire expanded inside him. "Physically, you're stronger. You don't look quite so fragile now. And look at how many times you've taken a stand against me. I'll bet you never fought with your ex-husband like that."

"No," she admitted quietly. She tilted her head to the side, allowing his fingers to brush the sensitive skin at the base of her neck. "Gary and I never fought. We discussed. And then we did everything his way."

"See, you're definitely making progress. You haven't done a thing I've said since you got here. And you possess a fine, forceful vocabulary." He was pleased by the chuckle she emitted.

"And you call that progress?" she asked doubtfully.

"Certainly." With gentle fingers he gathered her hair together in one hand and drew it away. Bending, he nuzzled his lips against her warm nape. "Your ex-husband is a fool, Kathleen," he murmured against her warm skin. "There are few things more beautiful than you sparking with temper."

She went very still against him and then pulled away. He dropped his hands to his sides and watched her warily as she moved down the steps. "Would you get my horse, please," she asked with overt politeness.

Her tone made it perfectly clear that the temperature had just dropped about twenty degrees. Casually, he crossed his arms over his chest and leaned against the railing. "Not just yet."

She turned to him then, her eyes red-rimmed from recent tears, but shooting sparks now. "I want to go home, Cody. Now."

"Why are you upset?"

She stared at him defiantly, but didn't speak. He saw the uncertainty hovering just below the anger. Finally, she let out a sharp breath and snapped, "I know I'm not beautiful, and I'd appreciate it if you'd save your careless compliments for your friendly red head."

"I don't have a friendly red head," he denied easily. "And I think you are beautiful."

She made a disgusted noise and looked away. "Would you just get my horse?"

"Who told you you weren't beautiful?" he challenged softly. "The same man who told you you have no talent?"

Her head jerked up and she blinked as if dazed by the thought. He came slowly down the steps, watching as she carefully analyzed his words. When he stopped in front of her, she looked up at him, her eyes filled with confusion and caution.

He reached up and gently framed her face between his hands. "Everything he told you is a lie, Kathleen. You are a beautiful, capable, and talented woman. And I'm not the only one who thinks so."

Emotion pooled in her eyes as he bent toward her. His mouth brushed hers lightly before coming back to settle into the kiss. Her hands came up and she dug her fingers into his forearms. He felt the moisture of her tears against his skin. He was tempted to deepen the kiss to a level guaranteed to drive all thought from her mind but him. Some instinct told him, however, that she needed tenderness a whole lot more than passion right now.

When he raised his head and looked down into her eyes, he still saw the doubt. Anger shot through him, but he reminded himself that the habits of a lifetime could not be reformed overnight. She needed time, and time was one thing he could afford to give her.

Her fingers were trembling when she reached up and wiped the smudges of moisture from his face. For a long moment her eyes searched his. Finally, she said in a broken whisper, "I don't want your pity, Cody."

He dropped his hands to his sides and took a step back. Disbelief rocked him and his frustration level nearly doubled. With a shake of his head, he reached out and firmly cupped her chin in one hand. "If you think any of this has to do with pity, you've got an awful lot to learn about me. Rethink it, Kathleen, and see what you can come up with." He released her and turned away. "I'll bring the horses around."

Five

Cody's words echoed inside Kathleen's mind without pause for days. Sometimes she would almost convince herself that he had said the words just to make her feel better. Then she'd remember the intensity in his eyes when he'd told her to rethink it, and she wouldn't be sure. The man was messing with her mind, and she didn't know how to deal with him.

Not that there had been much dealing to do. She'd seen him several times since the day at his ranch, but never for more than a few minutes at a time. She wondered if he was giving her space to consider his words, or if he needed the space himself.

Kathleen had had little experience with men. She'd married Gary when she was eighteen and there had been no real boyfriends before him. She was lost trying to define the strange sensations that Cody stirred inside her. It was tempting just to call it sexual attraction, but she had a hard time with that definition since sex had never been much of an earth shattering experience for her. Cody frightened her. A simple kiss with him was a mind altering experience. And an addictive one if she chose to be brutally honest with herself. She wanted Cody to kiss her again. She wanted to fully explore the emotions he'd awakened in her.

But what did he want? She didn't have a clue. He seemed determined not to push her in one direction or another. It almost seemed as if this attraction between them was something he was dealing with because he had to, not because he wanted to. She knew without a doubt that she annoyed him. But it wasn't annoyance that had generated the tenderness he'd shown her.

With a sigh, Kathleen stepped out onto the porch and sat down on the top step. It was growing late and most of the activity had ceased on the ranch. A light still glowed in the bunkhouse and a few of the cabins still showed signs of movement, but for the most part everyone had turned in for the day.

The sky was clear, and the stars were breathtaking in their number. A short distance away, Jon and the twins were tracking some mysterious celestial body with the help of a telescope he'd set up.

Kathleen smiled as she listened to their voices. Even Heather seemed to have put aside her sulkiness for the moment. Kathleen suspected it was Jon's attention that was momentarily filling the void Gary had left in Heather's life. It was obvious to everyone that Jon adored both of his nieces.

Time was passing quickly. They'd been on the ranch just over a month and the summer was slipping away. Kathleen was aware that there were decisions she had to make regarding her life. But she still wasn't sure what she wanted to do. No magical answers had come to her in the last few weeks.

She heard Jon suggest it was time to call it a day. Surprisingly, there was very little grumbling as the girls packed up the telescope and carried it toward the house.

"Thanks, Uncle Jon," Holly said as she reached up to kiss his cheek. She bent then and kissed her mother. "Good night, Mom."

"Good night, you two."

Heather bent for a quick kiss before following her sister inside.

Jon sat down on the step beside Kathleen and stretched his legs out. "They're great kids, Katie. You've done a good job raising them."

She wondered if he had any idea how much his praise meant to her. "Thanks. I think they're pretty special. It was nice to hear Heather without the sarcasm she's been carrying around the last year or so."

"She'll be okay. She'll always march to a slightly different beat, but she'll eventually outgrow the resentment she feels toward you." He reached out and squeezed her hand. "Has Gary returned your call yet?"

She shook her head. "He either doesn't want to talk to me or he hasn't gotten home yet." She shrugged. "If I don't hear from him, I'll call again tomorrow and leave another message on his machine."

"Have you decided what you're going to do?" Jon asked, looking out into the darkness. "You and Holly seem happy here. I'm not sure if Heather doesn't like it here, or if she's determined not to like it anywhere right now."

"She's already told me she won't stay here. She said she'd go to live with Gary." Kathleen looked over at her brother. "What do you think are the chances of that happening?"

"He'll break her heart when he refuses."

Solemnly, Kathleen nodded. "And she'll blame it all on me." Sighing, she drew her knees up and wrapped her arms around them. "I don't know what's best, Jon. There are so many things to think about. I can't just stay here and live off you. I need to get a job of some kind."

"From what I've seen and heard, you and the girls are real handy to have around. You're not living off me, Katie. Everybody knows you already pull your weight around here. Let me put you on the payroll."

She shook her head. "That's not the answer, Jon."

"Why not?" he challenged. "Earl told me you helped him groom some of the horses the other morning. I know how much you've helped Mattie in the dining hall. Louella told me you've taken it upon yourself to handle the incoming and outgoing mail, and that you can clean a cabin faster and better than anyone on staff. I've also had several compliments from folks regarding the friendly Kathleen who's been answering my phone and taking my messages." He arched a brow. "Have I missed anything?"

"I have to keep busy." It was the only explanation she offered him.

"Busy? You're a regular whirlwind of activity. Why don't you let me pay you for all you do?"

"You pay me with room and board right now."

He blew out a frustrated breath. "You're a stubborn woman, Katie. You need to realize there aren't a lot of jobs available in Wolfe Creek."

She nodded. "I've thought of that. Do you suppose I'd have better luck finding a job in Bozeman?"

"Bozeman is almost an hour away," he protested.

"We could live there, too."

Jon looked at her a long moment before shrugging lightly. "Bozeman is a great town. You could probably find something there."

"Maybe I'll check it out early next week."

He pushed to his feet and turned to look down at her. "If it's what you want to do, I won't argue with you," he said quietly. "But please remember that I have a legitimate job for you right here. Okay?"

She smiled up at him. "Okay. Thank you."

"Sure." He gave her one last searching look before climbing the steps to disappear inside.

Kathleen's trip to Bozeman the following Wednesday was not exactly encouraging. If she wanted to work for minimum wage, she could find any number of jobs. But minimum wage would not support her and the girls. She found herself hopelessly under qualified for the jobs that paid more. She didn't have the experience or the education most of them required. She was sure, however, that she could master some of the jobs, especially the clerical and secretarial ones, if someone would just give her a chance. Unfortunately, no one had seemed inclined to give her a trial period to prove herself.

Kathleen returned to the ranch more than a little dispirited. In addition to nursing a bruised ego, she was also bone-weary tired. She couldn't wait to get out of the navy suit and pumps she was wearing. Sweats and sneakers sounded like heaven.

She had barely parked the van and cut the engine before Heather was there waiting for her. Kathleen noticed her daughter's bright smile first thing. Something had obviously pleased the child.

"Daddy called," Heather announced as Kathleen slammed the van door shut. "Guess where he's been?"

"I wouldn't know." She made a conscious effort to keep her tone neutral. "Where?"

"Paris! He and Jackie were there for two weeks. He said he brought back something special for me and Holly."

Kathleen wondered why it still hurt. Gary had never had the time or the inclination to travel when they'd been married. Actually, he'd never been inclined to do much of anything that would have made her or the girls happy. It seemed that keeping Jackie happy had turned into a top priority for him. "Did he say what it was?"

"No. He's saving it for a surprise when we get home." With that bit of information, Heather turned and started for the dining hall. "I'm going to go tell Holly."

"How long ago did he call?"

"Just a few minutes. I hung up about five minutes before you pulled in."

Kathleen watched her daughter skip off before hurrying toward the house. If she was lucky, maybe she could catch Gary. And if she was really lucky, maybe he'd be relaxed following his vacation and more flexible than usual. A wry smile curved her lips as she went into Jon's study. If her job hunt was any indication, luck was not exactly following her around today.

She bit her lip nervously as she dialed Gary's number. He answered on the third ring.

"Hi, Gary. It's Kathleen."

"Ah, you've returned. Holly said she didn't know where you'd gone."

How typical, she thought. No greeting. Just thinly veiled disapproval. "I had some errands to run," she explained smoothly. "And you were talking to Heather, not Holly."

"I know that," he said instantly. "I just mixed up the names. What did you want?"

She leaned back against Jon's desk and quickly gathered her thoughts. "We need to talk about some things," she started. "The girls get upset when you don't call. Especially Heather. She misses you."

"And Holly doesn't?" he countered immediately.

"Yes, I'm sure she does, but not like Heather. You didn't come by to see them before we left and you haven't called since we arrived here. You need to contact them without me being the one to arrange it."

"I'm sure you can explain to them about the demands of my job."

She took a deep breath and let it out slowly. "Yes, I can, but I don't want to. You keep putting me in the middle, Gary, and it's not fair. They're your children, too."

"Kathleen, you're being silly." The impatience in his voice sounded clearly across the telephone line. It was the tone of voice she'd grown to hate over the years. Somehow by using it he always made her feel like the one at fault. She twisted the phone cord and reminded herself firmly that he no longer had any power to make her feel anything she didn't want to feel.

"I'm not being silly," she insisted. "Heather is having a hard time with all that's happened. She needs your attention now more than ever. She's . . . she's been giving me some trouble."

"It's your responsibility to keep them in line," he reminded her sharply.

She felt her temper spark. Years of conditioning had her automatically clamping down on it. And then she reminded herself that she didn't have to back down now. This man's opinion of her no longer mattered. She was free to respond any way she wanted to.

"I may have custody, but you're still their father. You have responsibilities, too."

"Fine. When you return home, I'll try to see more of them."

"I've decided to stay in Montana." She was startled by the declaration. She wasn't aware that she had consciously made the decision to stay. But now that she'd made the announcement it felt right. Staying was what she wanted and needed.

Silence stretched over the line. "As I said, when you come home. . . ."

"You're not listening," she interrupted. "I have decided to stay and start over here. There's nothing for me in Chicago."

"How can you even consider something so stupid?" he asked mildly, as if she were a child. "You're just being emotional and immature. I'm sure once you get back to familiar surroundings you'll forget all about this foolish idea. I'll plan on seeing you and the girls on Saturday. We'll work everything out then."

Kathleen laughed. She couldn't help herself. Here he was going on, arranging things to suit himself, completely dismissing her as stupid and foolish and immature. He was responding as he always had. The only difference was, he didn't know who he was dealing with now. And, honestly, neither did she.

"What's so funny?" he demanded, actually sounding annoyed.

"You are," she answered bluntly. "I'm not coming back, Gary. Not this Saturday or any other day. The days that you can tell me what to do are over. I'm doing what I want to do. I want to stay in Montana. I am going to stay in Montana. This is home now."

"So you're just going to uproot the girls with no thought to their feelings? What a caring mother you are, Kathleen."

She sighed softly. True to old patterns, he was changing his strategy. If he couldn't coerce her, he'd always been able to make her feel guilty to the core. "Holly is thrilled with the idea. I won't lie to you about Heather. She isn't happy. But she hasn't been happy about anything for a long time."

"She sounded fine when I talked to her."

"That's because she was talking to you. She misses you. You've got to have more contact with her, and Holly, too."

"And how can I do that, Kathleen, when you're two thousand miles away?"

"Well, there's always the phone. You're a pilot. From what Heather told me, you're traveling quite a lot these days with Jackie."

"Kathleen. . . ."

She heard the warning in his voice and joyfully ignored it. She felt a stab of satisfaction, knowing her jab had hit its mark. "Or the girls could always visit you," she finished.

There was a long pause. "You mean stay here with me?" he asked incredulously.

"That's exactly what I mean, Gary. They are your daughters, for God's sake. Why do you sound so surprised?"

"You know my schedule. Who would be with them when I was flying?"

"Well, it would be silly for them to come visit when you're flying," she returned smoothly. "They could come when you have vacation time to spend with them."

"Kathleen, this whole thing is nonsense. What do you think you're accomplishing by staying in Montana? It makes no sense. Why cut yourself off from everything that's familiar to you and the girls?"

"Why, Gary? Because I want to. I like it here."

She heard his scathing laugh. "You would. If you're doing this to get back at me, it's not going to work."

Was there no end to this man's ego? "This has absolutely nothing to do with you and everything to do with me. The only reason I called was to let you know my plans and to ask you to help me with Heather. I can see I wasted my money."

"I can't very well help you if you're there and I'm here. Now if you'll just come home. . . ."

"Montana is home now. If you don't want to help me, just say so. If I can't count on you for any kind of emotional support, I prefer to know now."

"What the hell is the matter with you? I don't appreciate this new attitude of yours."

"I don't give a damn what you appreciate," she shot back. "I've got a problem and you're part of it. Either help me solve it or stay out of my way while I do."

Silence hummed between them. For a moment she thought he might have hung up on her. Finally, he said very softly, "So you've grown claws since you went away, Kathleen? It's pretty easy to be assertive when you're two thousand miles away."

"Yeah, maybe you're right," she said impatiently, running a hand through her hair. "But I'm not the issue here. Your daughters are. You might as well know right now that Heather has already told me she wants to come live with you if I decide to stay. Are you prepared to deal with her when she calls?"

"Damn it, Kathleen, we can avoid all this foolishness if you'd listen to reason. Give the girls a few more years in Chicago and then they'll be old enough that you can go anywhere in the world you want. What's the big attraction out there anyway? Did you latch on to a cowboy or something?"

Her temper snapped. "This conversation is over. Call me back when you want to discuss the relevant issues regarding your children." With shaking fingers she slammed the receiver down.

She stood for a moment, trying to control the trembling that set in almost instantly. Warring urges, one to laugh and one to cry, tugged her in opposite directions. When the ringing of the phone pierced the silence, she jumped, but didn't reach to answer. After four rings Jon's answering machine came on with his recorded message. She listened, clasping her hands tightly together in front of her. She felt no surprise when Gary's voice filled the room.

"Kathleen, I know you're still there. Pick up the damned phone. Now, Kathleen. I've had enough of your foolishness." He paused and she stood staring at the machine with a kind of hypnotic fascination. "Stop this right now, Kathleen, and talk to me. I know you're standing right there." He paused again. She didn't move. She heard him mutter one final expletive before the connection was broken.

Relief washed over her like warm heat. A smile curved her lips and laughter bubbled up inside. She'd just snapped a cord that had been binding her for too many years, and it felt wonderful.

"You're one tough lady."

Kathleen jumped and turned toward the door. Jon was leaning in the doorway, amusement lighting his eyes.

He stepped into the room. "I heard the phone and rushed in to answer it. Then I saw you standing there obviously enjoying your ex's tirade."

"I was." She laughed, feeling suddenly very self-conscious. "I think I won this battle. At least I took my stand and didn't back down."

Jon nodded. "Good for you." He studied her face, taking in the excited flush. "Victory agrees with you."

"It feels wonderful. I feel like I've just freed myself of a burden that has been weighing me down for years." She frowned and looked at him. "Does that sound really strange?"

"No." He shook his head and smiled. "I think you're well on your way to getting rid of all the excess baggage Gary saddled you with."

"I think you're right," she said with new-found confidence. She glanced down at her watch. "I better get changed so I can help Mattie in the dining hall."

"Don't worry about it tonight. Olan is out at the stables. He said he'd like to talk to you."

"Okay." She felt like she owed Olan and Jenny an apology for the way she'd run out during her visit two weeks ago. "Let me go change, then I'll be down."

"You don't owe us an explanation, Kathleen," Olan said gently, "or an apology. Jenny and I understand."

"Well, thank you. I just feel very foolish."

"There's no need."

They were walking away from the stables along a path that led behind the outbuildings and toward a stocked pond on the other side of a hill. Early evening shadows stretched out before them, adding a slight chill to the air. Kathleen was glad for the warmth of the yellow cable-knit sweater and jeans she wore.

"Jon mentioned that you went job hunting in Bozeman today," Olan said casually.

"I went hunting, but I didn't find anything."

"No luck at all?"

"Not unless I want to make a career out of flipping hamburgers." She gave a rueful laugh. "I'm afraid I've set my sights a little higher than that. However, with my lack of skills, I may have to settle for a whole lot less."

"What would you say if I told you I might have a job for you?"

Her steps slowed and she cast him a suspicious glance. "I'd say that would be a pretty big coincidence."

He stopped and met her gaze directly. "Don't look at me like I've been in cahoots with your brother. He doesn't know why I wanted to talk to you. I haven't even mentioned this idea to Cody or Jenny. I wanted to talk to you first."

Some of the wariness left her features. He arched a brow, looking suddenly just like his son. "Will you listen with an open mind?" he asked.

"Yes, of course. I don't mean to be so suspicious. It's just that with my lack of skills, I can't imagine what I could legitimately do for you."

He smiled gently and shook his head. "Kathleen, you haven't even begun to tap into your real potential." She frowned as he turned to start walking again. "Let's keep going," he said. "The pond is one of my favorite spots."

She moved along beside him, her mind jumping from one question to another. He seemed to be considering his words carefully, so she didn't want to push him. But she was very curious about this job of his.

"Several years ago I considered opening a museum featuring western art. Not just mine, but others in this area. It was my wife's idea. When Sara died, I couldn't go on with the plans. First of all, because it was her dream. And second, because I just didn't have the time to oversee such a project. I also didn't know anyone who would be willing or capable of putting in the time and effort Sara would have." He paused and looked over at Kathleen. "Until I met you."

Kathleen stopped in her tracks and stared at him. "You've got to be kidding. I don't know anything about setting up a museum and running it. My volunteer work wasn't quite that extensive."

"So you're turning down my offer without considering it?"

"Olan, I'm not qualified."

"If I wanted someone with glowing qualifications I'd have no trouble finding them, Kathleen. I could have put the word out and have qualified candidates lined up for a mile. But that's not what

I'm looking for. I'm looking for someone whose heart would be in it. I want someone who sees the soul of the art. A person doesn't study to achieve that, Kathleen. It's something they're born with. The mechanics can always be learned." He tilted his head slightly and studied her a long moment. "You've got the heart. Just as Sara did. I'm convinced that you have the intelligence necessary to learn what you need to know about the rest. I guess what I have to wonder is if you've got the courage to take the challenge."

Kathleen turned her attention toward the pond. Sunlight glinted off the glassy surface. "I guess I have to wonder the same thing," she admitted quietly.

"I wouldn't have made the offer if I didn't believe in you, Kathleen. I think you can do this, and I think you can do it well."

She looked back at him wondering what he saw in her that inspired his trust. Didn't he see the weakness and fear that plagued her? Didn't he see all the flaws in her character?

A ghost of a smile played around his mouth. "And you thought I was going to offer you some cushy job just because I felt sorry for you," he chided gently. "I'll be going to New York tomorrow for a few days. Why don't you take that time to think about my offer? I'll call you when I get back."

She nodded mutely.

"Okay," he agreed. "I'll see you in a few days."

He turned and set a leisurely pace back along the path they'd just come. Kathleen watched him go. She needed time to think. Slowly, she walked down to the pond.

Six

Kathleen was sure that she'd never had as much to think about in her entire life as she had since arriving in Montana. The Washington men alone seemed hell-bent on keeping her mind constantly in motion. First the son, and now the father. One issuing kisses and the other challenges. She wasn't sure she could keep up with either of them. But oh, how she was tempted to try.

She sat at the edge of the pond, watching as the sun slowly descended toward a distant mountain peak. Occasionally, a fish would jump, disturbing the peaceful setting. She let the tranquility soothe her as her mind turned in slow, steady circles.

A museum featuring Olan Washington's work. The idea kept coming back to her, enticing and teasing. The thought of it excited her. But she really had no experience. She had, though, seen how efficiently the Wainright Museum had been run. She wasn't completely ignorant. But she'd be responsible for this museum. Amazingly, that thought didn't terrify her as much as it had thirty minutes ago.

It was important that she think rationally without her emotions stirring things up. The first thing she needed to recognize was the fact that this was Olan's project, not hers. He would obviously provide the financial backing and the details of how he'd want things set up. All she would do was oversee the project and then see that things ran smoothly once the museum was open.

The more she thought about it, the more appealing it became.

"I can almost see the wheels turning."

Startled, she jerked around to find Cody standing directly behind her. She'd been so involved in her thoughts that she hadn't heard him approach. "You scared me," she accused.

"Sorry, but I didn't sneak up on you. I made enough noise that most people would have heard." He frowned and studied her face. "What are you thinking so hard about?"

"Life," she said vaguely. "What are you doing out here?"

"Looking for you. I'd like you to take a ride with me."

"Take a ride with you?" she repeated warily.

"Don't look so suspicious," he teased. "I'm not planning to abduct you. You'll be safe."

She truly doubted that. Being close to this man seemed like a very dangerous place to be. She pushed to her feet and turned to face him. "Where are we going?"

"I want to show you the place Mom bought for the museum."

Kathleen frowned at him. "Olan said he hadn't told you about his plans to go ahead with the museum."

"He hasn't told me," Cody assured her. "But I knew the day you were at the ranch that he would ask you to oversee it. You were so caught up in your own feelings about the paintings you were describing that you didn't see the light that came on inside of him."

"I haven't agreed to do this, Cody," she warned him. "I don't have the qualifications for this job."

He shook his head and slowly closed the distance between them. "Neither did my mother. Kathleen, she didn't even have a high school education. She was forced to drop out of school when she was sixteen because her mother became ill and she was needed at home to care for her five younger brothers and sisters. My mother did not have a formal education. All she had was a love for people and art and history. And a dream to bring all three together in one place as a tribute to those who put their heart and soul into their work." He reached up and brushed his knuckles against her cheek. "Can you honestly tell me you can't match her qualifications?"

He wasn't wearing his hat, leaving his features free of the concealing shadows she had grown used to. Kathleen stared up into his face, mesmerized by the gleam of certainty in his eyes. He believed in her. She was stunned by how much his support meant to her. He smiled, a slow curving of his mouth, and she felt her heart lurch against her ribs. In that instant she knew there was more brewing between them than just his support of her. She felt as if she was standing on shifting ground. Her own emotions were a jumbled mess, and she had no idea what his feelings were.

"Come on," he said quietly. "I'm not asking you to make any kind of decision now. Just go with me to see the place."

In the end she didn't even hesitate. With a sinking feeling in the pit of her stomach she had to admit to herself that she'd probably follow this man to the moon if he asked.

Cody turned off the main highway leading into Wolfe Creek and onto a rutted dirt drive. He made a valiant effort to miss the biggest craters in the road. It was the countless smaller ones that were pitching the truck to and fro. Kathleen's fingers clenched around the armrest on the passenger door, trying to keep herself steady.

Cody shot her a quick grin. "First thing we'll have to do is get some gravel out here."

The drive curved around through a stand of pine trees momentarily plunging the interior of the truck into darkness. When they emerged on the other side, Kathleen couldn't help the small gasp that escaped her. She blinked once and then just stared. There before her, with the last rays of the day's light glowing softly upon it, was a beautiful two-story colonial mansion. It sat majestically on a slight rise with a row of blue and gray mountains as a backdrop.

Cody followed the circular drive around and stopped in front of the main entrance. He shut the engine off and looked over at her. He felt a certain smug satisfaction at the look of awe on her face. Without speaking, she pushed her door open and stepped out.

"It needs a fresh coat of paint," he noted as he came around the front of the truck. He stood back and studied the peeling paint and faded shutters, trying to determine how many gallons of paint he'd have to buy.

"It's fantastic," Kathleen breathed. She ran her gaze over the six columns supporting the full-length portico roof. Even without fresh paint it was an impressive sight.

"Wait until you see inside," Cody said as he moved toward the double wide entrance, key in hand. He pushed the door open and reached inside to flip on a light before gesturing for Kathleen to enter first.

She stepped into the open two-story foyer and caught her breath. Above her was a crystal chandelier that seemed to be dripping with diamonds. Directly beside her was a curved staircase that led to an overlooking balcony. Even with the floors stripped bare and the walls patched and primed for paint, it was easy to see how elegant this entry would eventually be.

"As you can see, we stopped in the middle of renovation," Cody said. "I've worked at it some off and on over the years but there's a lot still to be done."

She looked over at him. "How did your mother die?" she asked gently.

"Car accident." He reached around her and closed the front door.

"How long ago did it happen?"

"It'll be four years this December." He moved to turn away, but was stopped by the feel of her hand connecting with his. Her simple touch seemed to travel up his arm and straight to his heart. When he lifted his gaze to meet hers, he felt as if the world came to a dead halt. Suddenly there were no walls between them. He looked into her eyes and saw a wellspring of emotion just waiting to be tapped. It stunned him to realize how badly he wanted to be the one to do it.

"Let's look at the rest," he said, his voice low and strained. She started to withdraw her hand, but his fingers tightened around it. He led her through a wide, arched doorway to the right and into what was once a formal living room. With the flip of a switch, dim light chased away the shadows.

The long room was in the same condition as the foyer. Tall windows gave a view of the front yard and a brick fireplace was centered on the end wall.

"The downstairs is a circular floor plan," Cody explained as he led her toward another arched doorway. He found another light switch. "This would have been the dining room." He pointed toward a set of French doors on the back wall. "Those lead out to a porch that runs the length of the house."

He gave her a minute to look around before proceeding. "This room was a large eat-in kitchen," he said, as he stepped through another archway. "As you can see we've completely gutted it."

"Why didn't you finish in honor of your mother's memory?"

"I thought we would." Cody paused and carefully gathered his thoughts. The time following his mother's death had been an extremely dark period for him. "Dad took her death hard. He closed himself off. The day of the funeral he closed his studio and didn't open it again for nearly two years. He just stopped creating."

"How sad," Kathleen murmured.

"Mom had created a gallery at the house. The paintings in it were ones she couldn't bear to part with. Dad used to tease her, telling her that we were all going to starve unless she let him sell his work. She told him that he made enough on his commissioned work to take care of us. That gallery was always open to guests who stayed with us. Mom would walk through with them and she'd always pick a couple of paintings to tell a special story about. I can't tell you how many times I'd seen people mesmerized by her voice and tale. She brought those scenes alive for people." He looked at Kathleen closely. "I've never heard anyone else do that until you did the other day when you were talking about the Custer battlefield paintings. Those paintings had been in the private collection and were two of Mom's favorites. If you hadn't become so embarrassed, you would have seen the absolute awe on my father's face. And probably on mine, too."

She dropped her gaze, but not before he saw the tears shimmering in her eyes. He wanted to hold her. Not so much to comfort her as to seek comfort for himself. He didn't understand this need that had begun to grow in him from their very first meeting. He'd never felt anything like it before. Desire was a simple emotion and one he had experience with. What he was feeling for Kathleen was not simple. It was dangerous. And he was precariously close to losing what little control he had.

Deliberately, he moved to put some distance between them. He released her hand and instantly regretted it. He knew it was a foolish reaction, but he couldn't help it. To check the urge he felt to reach for her again, he slid his hands into the pockets of his jeans.

Kathleen lifted her gaze to his, the trace of tears gone. "He couldn't bear to finish it, could he," she said softly.

"No. To my knowledge, he hasn't set foot in this place since she died. At one point shortly after the funeral, he came up with a plan to sell or donate all the paintings in Mom's gallery and then sell this place, too. That's how the Wainright Museum ended up with the Custer battlefield paintings. Those were the only two to get away before I asked him to stop. I think his theory was if he erased all traces of the things Mom cherished, then he wouldn't hurt as much. But I knew he'd eventually want to finish what she'd started." He paused and studied Kathleen a long moment. "Even now, I don't think he can come in here and do this himself. But he obviously feels that he can trust you to do this for him."

Kathleen turned away abruptly and walked toward the windows. "What about Jenny?" she asked. "Why not her?"

"He met Jenny about a year ago, and I know he loves her. But she's the total opposite of my mother. Not only is she a generation younger, she comes from a very privileged background. Jenny admires what my father does, but she doesn't understand it. To her, he just paints pretty pictures, and that's as deep as she wants to get." When Kathleen turned to frown at him over her shoulder, he added, "I don't mean to take anything away from her. She's been great for Dad, but I think he consciously chose someone who would never remind him of Mom." He shrugged helplessly. "I don't know, maybe I'm wrong. But I do know Jenny doesn't have the love for art that my mother did. Or you do."

Kathleen sighed and turned back to look out the window. Absently, she reached up and began to rub her arms through the thick fabric of her sweater. Night had fallen, and Cody could see her reflection in the glass of the windows almost as clearly as a mirror. The indecision and uncertainty were easy enough to read.

"I'm afraid you and Olan might be expecting too much of me," she said in a voice barely audible. "What if we get into this and it becomes apparent that I can't handle it?"

"I'll help you," he offered, immediately wondering if he had taken leave of his senses. Here he was offering to jump feet first into a situation that could prove to be his downfall.

She shook her head. "You're not listening to me. What if I can't do it? What if we get halfway into it and you realize I don't have the kind of instincts you think I do? What if I'm not like your mother?"

"I didn't tell you about my mother to put pressure on you, Kathleen," he said quietly. "I just wanted you to have the background of this project. My father has not made this offer to any other person. Obviously, he sees something in you that he believes in. I agree with him."

"What if you're both wrong?" she whispered.

He moved slowly across the room until he was standing beside her. He peered down at her, but she refused to meet his eyes. "Is it that you're afraid of failing, Kathleen," he asked gently, "or that you're afraid of trying?"

"I don't know," she admitted openly. She turned to him then, her eyes so eloquent that he wanted nothing more than to drown in the mysterious blue-gray pools. Emotion swelled within his chest, but he felt powerless to move either away or toward her. She had captured him with some kind of magic spell. Probably a magic she had no idea she possessed.

"No one has ever believed in me," she said flatly.

"Then it's time someone did. The only way you can fail is if you don't try."

"I know. But I'm still afraid."

He smiled. "It's okay to be afraid. I'll help you all I can."

She stared up into his face, studying him as if trying to see behind his words. Tentatively, she reached up and laid her hand against his upper arm. Her fingers kneaded gently, testing the strength there. Her touch seared directly through the cotton sleeve of his shirt to burn his skin. Breathing suddenly became a difficult task. He watched her, drawn by the open honesty in her eyes. Logically, he knew he needed to move away.

He stepped closer, his hands coming to rest lightly at her waist. The sweater was rough beneath his palms and he itched to push it aside and seek the silky flesh beneath. He lifted one hand and curved it along the column of her throat. Beneath his fingers he felt her pulse beating an unsteady rhythm. She drew in a quiet breath and his gaze was drawn to her mouth. His thumb came up to trace lightly over the full bottom lip. She tilted her head back and let her eyes drift closed.

Cody felt the silent invitation shoot straight to the very center of his soul. His hand slid to the small of her back and he shifted slightly, bringing her body flush with his own. The lines of her body were cushioned by the thickness of her sweater. He nearly groaned with frustration. He wanted to feel her against him. He wanted to learn and trace every curve and valley of her. He wanted to taste and touch without restriction.

He bent toward her, teasing her lips with the tip of his tongue. He tempted, but never took sweet possession of her mouth. When he finally lifted his head, her lids slowly lifted. He looked down into eyes of midnight blue. Desire flared within those smokey depths, sending answering flames licking through his own veins.

"Cody. . . ."

Her voice was the barest of whispers; his name a prayer, a plea, a promise. Her arms slipped up over his shoulders until her fingers dipped into the hair at the back of his head. The slight pressure she exerted was barely felt as he leaned toward her and she raised up on her toes to meet him.

The explosion was instantaneous and rocked him like nothing ever had. His mouth slanted over hers, hungry and searching for answers to questions that hadn't been spoken. When she opened to him, he moaned softly and deepened the kiss, tasting and taking, and wanting so much more. He felt her fingers bite into his shoulders as she clung to him in the face of the storm. And still he sought more, pulling her into the vortex of swirling and undefined emotions.

Time might have stopped or raced forward. He had no way of knowing. Mountains could have crumbled to the ground and he wouldn't have known or cared. His senses were all wrapped up in this woman who responded with such an unrestricted passion that it threatened to bring him to his knees. Her scent, her taste, her texture seduced him until everything else just faded away. There was only her and him and emotions that were fast approaching a point of no return.

It was too much. The single thought crept through the fog in Cody's mind once before becoming lost. It came back with a sharper clarity, demanding his attention. He yearned to ignore it, but the warning was joined by a cacophony of others just as insistent. It was too strong, too hot. She was too vulnerable. He was too needy. And it was too soon for either of them.

With a supreme effort he lifted his head and looked down into her face. He nearly decided the hell with it. Her cheeks were flushed, her lips swollen and soft from the pressure of his. Her eyes were dark and inviting. He groaned as he wrapped his arms around her and pushed her head against his chest.

"God, Katie," he murmured against her hair. "You pack quite a punch."

She didn't answer verbally, but he felt her arms go around his waist. She trembled, and he ran his hand up and down her back in a soothing rhythm. He was still trying to get his own emotions under control. What he had just experienced was indescribable. There were not enough adjectives in the English language to do it justice. He'd just stepped into a fantastic world filled with delightful mysteries. A world he'd only gotten a taste of. A world he wanted to explore thoroughly with Kathleen. Only Kathleen.

He closed his eyes and drew in a deep breath. He was in deep trouble, no doubt about it. He was close to losing his heart to a woman who was far from ready to accept it. She didn't need the additional complications he would bring to her life. She was healing, and he had no right to interfere with the process. Her entire life had been spent in the shadows of others: first her father and then her husband.

Cody knew he never wanted to overshadow her, but he also knew his instinctive need to protect her might be viewed as such a maneuver. He knew the best thing he could do for both of them was back off and let her set her own pace, find her own rhythm. He needed to hold onto his heart a while longer. When he offered it to her, he wanted to be sure she was ready to accept it. There was no room for halfway measures with Kathleen. It would have to be all or nothing.

She stirred against him and he loosened his hold. Slowly, she pushed away until she no longer rested against his body. She slid him a tentative glance and he smiled, liking the dazed look that still lingered in her eyes. She turned away and out of his arms. He tried not to think about how useless they felt without her in them.

"I'm. . . ." Her voice cracked and she took a deep breath before starting again. "I'm not quite sure what just happened."

He chuckled softly. "What just happened is something we've been working up to for weeks."

She frowned and his grin widened. "What we experienced was just a taste, Katie. Based on that taste, I think we can safely assume that the full ride is going to be out of this world."

She shook her head. "I've never been very good at that sort of thing," she said uneasily.

"Oh, really?" He crossed to her, feeling a flare of disgust for the man who had so completely brainwashed her. "Maybe you should just make me a list of all the things he told you you weren't good at. Then I can just go down that list and one by one prove to you how wrong he is."

"No, it's true," she insisted nervously. "I just never enjoyed it much and I've never. . . ." Her voice trailed off and she looked away, her cheeks flaming.

He reached out and framed her face between his hands. Gently, he lifted her face to his. "You will," he assured her firmly. "I'll guarantee it. It's never been you, Kathleen. Never. When we make love it'll be because you want to. When we make love, you'll discover exactly what he cheated you out of." He studied her face, seeing how badly she wanted to believe. It was just about equal to how badly he wanted to be the one to convince her. A slow smile curved his mouth. "When we make love, Kathleen," he said, his voice purposely husky, "you'll want to do it again. And again. And again."

As if mesmerized by his voice, she swayed toward him, but he didn't succumb to the temptation. He bent and kissed her forehead tenderly before releasing her. "I think we better finish up here before your family begins to wonder what's happened to you."

She drew in a deep breath and nodded. "You're right. How much more is there?"

"Just two more rooms down here and the upstairs." He gestured toward an arched doorway and she preceded him on the rest of the tour.

Seven

Maybe it was just lust. Kathleen frowned, disliking the blunt, cold feeling the word conjured. It might have been a fair assessment on the surface, but it didn't come close to identifying all the emotions that had sizzled between her and Cody three days ago. There'd been more involved than just two people wanting to satisfy a sexual urge. There'd been some kind of connection on a deeper level.

She pulled another bed sheet from the dryer and began to fold it with quick, efficient movements. Maybe she was making too much out of it. Her hands stilled for a moment as her mind went back over the kiss. She remembered how easily she'd lost all concept of time or place. He had invaded all of her senses and she'd offered no resistance. Even now, days later and standing in the middle of the bright yellow laundry room, she felt her cheeks heat at the memory. Her unrepressed response had felt natural and necessary at the time. But it embarrassed her now. She knew the only reason they had not progressed to the next level of intimacy was because of Cody. He'd been the one to show the least bit of common sense. If he hadn't stopped. . . .

She swore softly under her breath and went back to folding sheets. "Admit it, Kathleen," she muttered. "You wanted the man, and you gave no thought to the consequences." And you still want him, a little voice accused inside her head.

She jerked another sheet from the dryer and shook it out with a vicious snap of her wrist. What was Cody thinking of her behavior? She cringed at the thought. He probably thought she was a sex-starved divorcée about to sink her hooks into his flesh. Well, he was wrong. She'd always told herself that when she finally left Gary, she'd never seek out another relationship. Sex was something she could definitely live without, and the idea of sharing her life with one special person was a myth as far as she was concerned. She didn't need anyone but herself.

She stacked the folded sheets on the long worktable and moved over to open the second dryer. She pulled out a tangle of towels and washcloths and began to fold them. She definitely was not looking for any kind of relationship with Cody. And if she was reading him right, he was just as anxious to steer clear of her. If he was looking for a quick tumble, he could forget about that, too. Sex didn't hold enough appeal for her to even consider it.

A sharp image of his body pressed close to hers flashed into her mind. She caught a surprised breath as sensation uncurled low in her stomach. Her sweater may have been thick when he'd held her, but there'd been no denying the hard lines of his body straining against hers. He'd wanted her, and he must have sensed her willingness. He must have known that she was past the point of protest. Why had he stopped?

Her hands slowed their movements until the task of folding towels was momentarily forgotten. She'd pegged him as just another overbearing male when she'd first come here. But she knew now she was wrong. He might be demanding and forceful at times, but he wasn't unfair or unkind. His actions were based on what he felt was right for the situation. And that probably explained why he'd stopped when he had.

Despite the passion that had flared between them, he'd held back, knowing that when the flames died away, they'd be left to deal with the tangled debris. He'd known that she wasn't ready for the kind of commitment their making love would signify. When they made love, he'd want them to be on equal ground. And so did she.

When they made love? Her eyes closed as a wave of anxiety washed over her. She couldn't deny it. She wanted to make love with Cody. Gary's cruel words still rang in her ears, but she pushed them aside. Cody was so far removed from her ex-husband that any comparison was foolish. Cody had stirred her soul with just a kiss. She wanted to believe she'd moved him in a similar way. She wanted to believe that it really hadn't been her lack of sensuality over the years that had led to such a mediocre love life with Gary. She wanted to believe she wasn't totally to blame for everything that had gone wrong.

"Mom!"

Holly's call snapped Kathleen back from her soul searching. She turned just as her daughter burst through the door and skidded to a halt beside her.

"Are you ready to go?" she asked breathlessly. "The bus is loading. Uncle Jon said to come on."

Kathleen looked around the room, realizing that if she hadn't been so caught up in her thoughts, she could have gotten all the laundry folded and put away. Now she'd have to finish up after they came back from town.

"Go ahead and finish if you want." At the sound of Cody's voice, both Holly and Kathleen turned toward the door. Instead of his usual work clothes, he was dressed in sharply pleated jeans and a burgundy and navy plaid shirt. He'd traded in his dusty Stetson for a spotless black one and the boots peeking out from the bottom of his jeans were highly polished.

He tipped his hat back and arched a brow. "I do clean up every now and then," he said dryly.

Kathleen blinked and then turned away abruptly. God, she'd been staring like a star struck teenager. What was it about this man that was forever throwing her off balance? To cover her embarrassment, she went back to folding towels.

"Mom, we need to go," Holly insisted.

"You go on," Cody said easily. "Your mom can ride with me."

Holly turned to her mother. "Is that okay with you?"

Kathleen hesitated and shot a quick look at Cody. "Don't you normally go on the bus?"

"No. When we take the bus, one of us always follows in the pickup just in case the bus has problems." He smiled slightly. "It's proven to be a practical approach to an old problem."

Kathleen nodded and turned to Holly. "Go ahead. Tell Jon I'll be coming with Cody."

"Got it." Holly dashed from the room.

"I'll only be a few minutes," Kathleen said as she went back to the job at hand.

"We have time," he said, as he walked toward her. "As slow as that bus goes, we'll be able to catch up easily."

Kathleen felt her stomach clench as he stopped beside her and reached out to lift a towel from the pile. She kept her head bent, but found herself distracted by the easy movements of his hands as he folded the piece of cotton. It was ridiculous, she scolded herself. Any man was capable of folding laundry. Why the sight of his hands performing the simple task would cause any kind of reaction in her was beyond comprehension. Unless it had something to do with wondering how those hands would feel on her bare skin.

Frantically, she pushed that thought away. She couldn't afford to think along those lines. It was too dangerous. He was too dangerous. But if he was so dangerous, then why had she allowed herself to be left alone with him? Now there was a million dollar question.

"If you don't relax, you're going to shatter into about a million pieces," he said quietly, breaking into her circling thoughts.

"I'm fine. I just want to get this done."

"It'll get done. Calm down."

She wished she could. There was something about him that made her so jittery she could barely hang onto the towels. His scent, the heat radiating from his body, seemed to reach out and wrap around her. For some reason she could not think clearly when he was this close. It was crazy.

"I've got an idea." His hand reached out and curved around the back of her neck. Instantly, her gaze flew up to his. He was smiling, a curious light in his eyes.

The air backed up in her lungs. She opened her mouth to speak, but nothing came out. He was bending toward her, his intent perfectly clear. Her eyes closed at the first brush of his lips on hers. She felt him draw back slightly and knew if she wanted, she could stop this right now. The situation was hers to control. All she had to do was step back or turn away.

His fingertips glided lightly up and down her neck. Her lids lifted, and she looked into eyes the color of shining emeralds. She saw the question there and knew he was waiting for her. Whatever happened next between them would be her choice. He wasn't pushing or pulling. He was merely waiting.

"You make me feel things I've never felt before." The admission tumbled out before she realized she was speaking out loud.

He smiled. "Good. Because you make me feel things I've never felt before."

She studied his face, wondering if he was teasing her. Was it possible? Could she stir feelings in him like she never had in Gary?

As she watched, the humor faded from his features. "Don't compare me to him, Kathleen," he murmured.

She shook her head. "You're nothing like him."

Her response seemed to satisfy him, but still the intensity stayed in his eyes. She wondered what he was searching for. What did he see when he studied her so thoroughly?

"Kiss me," he ordered quietly.

She stared at him wide-eyed as shock rolled through her. At first she thought he must be joking, but there was no laughter in his eyes. He'd taken a step back and was no longer touching her. He was watching her with a definite challenge in those green eyes.

"Cody, I . . ."

"No," he cut her off. "I don't want to hear any kind of excuse. Just kiss me the way you want to."

"When did I say I wanted to kiss you?" she retorted, trying to alleviate some of the panic she was feeling.

"You don't have to say it," he replied, his voice husky. "I can see it in your eyes when you look at me."

"I think you should think about getting glasses." She started to turn away, but his next words stopped her dead in her tracks.

"He's still controlling you, Kathleen, and you're letting him do it. Was it the rule that he always initiated any affection between you? He led and you were expected to follow?"

Anger burst bright inside her. He saw too much. She hated being so transparent. "Gary has no control over me." Her voice shook. She wondered who she was trying to convince; Cody or herself.

"You're lying. It's one thing to lie to me, but it's unforgivable that you're still lying to yourself."

"Who the hell do you think you are? You don't know enough about me or my life to pass any kind of judgment."

"I know a lot more than you're willing to admit. That's why you're angry with me now. You know I'm right. You may have taken some important steps away from his control, but he still stands as firmly between you and what you really want as he ever did. In your mind he's still calling the shots. He's still telling you what you can and you can't do. He's still telling you what you want and don't want. And the only reason he's still controlling you is because you're allowing him to. You're still his puppet and you know it."

The sound of her palm connecting with his cheek exploded in

the quiet room. Green eyes narrowed as a mocking smile tilted one side of his mouth. "Very impressive," he said flatly. "But I would have preferred the kiss."

Kathleen stared at him, appalled as the imprint of her hand became apparent on his cheek. "I don't recall asking your opinion regarding my personal life," she said dully.

"Please forgive me," he stated with exaggerated politeness. "Your point is well taken." With a slight nod of his head, he stepped around her. "If you still care to ride into town with me, I'll be leaving in five minutes."

She didn't turn to watch him go. Shock and fury trembled through her. She was shocked by her reaction to his words. Never had she struck out at another person as viciously as she had Cody. The fury came from deep within her and was painfully intense. But it wasn't directed at Cody. It was directed at herself. He'd been right, and she'd been too ashamed to admit it.

And now she was left to wonder if her pride had cost her the fragile friendship that had grown between them.

The Wolfe Creek Anniversary Celebration was without a doubt the biggest social event of the year. Festivities started at six in the morning with a pancake breakfast and officially ended just after dark with a huge fireworks display. In between, there were games for children and adults, rodeo events, arts and crafts displays and a stage set up on the town square for local talent to perform along with a platform for anyone who cared to dance. Added to this was enough food and drink to satisfy the entire county and anyone else who happened to wander through.

The thirty minute drive into town with Cody was as uncomfortable as Kathleen expected it to be. Tension hummed just below the surface, but neither of the two occupants of the truck seemed inclined to bridge the chasm that had opened between them. Kathleen knew she owed him an apology and had made the decision to deliver it before they reached town. But Cody had adopted a facade of cool courtesy, leaving her to feel that any apology she offered would slide right off him.

They arrived in time to gather outside the bus with the rest of the guests from the ranch. Jon let everyone know when and where they would meet for the trip home. When he finished, the crowd broke into smaller groups and wandered off in different directions.

Kathleen had fully expected Cody to go his own way. She wouldn't have blamed him if he had. When he didn't, she couldn't deny being both surprised and pleased.

"Well? Where do we start?" Heather looked to her uncle for direction.

He smiled. "Why don't we just mosey into town and see what kind of trouble we can get into?"

"Sounds good to me," Heather agreed immediately. She turned to grab her sister's arm. "Come on, Holly, let's go."

Jon slid a glance to his sister as the two girls started off. "Is it my imagination, or does it seem to you that Heather is actually looking forward to this?"

Kathleen chuckled. "I don't think it's your imagination."

"Maybe we're winning her over," Mattie offered.

"Maybe." Kathleen looked after her daughters, unexpectedly touched by the sight of them laughing together at some private joke. These kind of moments had been rare in the last year. Maybe it was true that time did indeed heal all wounds.

"We better get going or they'll leave us behind," Jon said. He reached for Mattie's hand and they followed the girls.

Kathleen felt Cody's gaze and turned to meet it. His expression was carefully guarded. "Do you mind if I join your group today?" he asked evenly.

She felt her heart squeeze tight. "Of course I don't mind." She looked up into his cool eyes, missing the warmth she was growing used to seeing there. "Cody, I. . . ."

"We better get going," he interrupted, stepping around her. "Believe it or not there's a lot to see."

Sighing, she turned to follow him.

Cody lifted the can of soft drink to his lips and drained the last drop of liquid from it as he leaned back in the metal chair and stretched his legs out. He set the empty can aside and absently began to turn it in slow circles. Then he watched as Kathleen whirled by again in the arms of the local rodeo hero.

Jealousy, was an unfamiliar emotion for Cody, but the notorious green-eyed monster was staring him straight in the face now. He'd hardly recognized it at first because he'd had so little experience with it. He'd never cared enough about anyone before for it to matter. Now it did. More than it should. More than he wanted to admit even to himself.

"If you continue to scowl like that, you're going to wear permanent lines into your face."

Cody looked up to find this bit of wisdom tossed out by Jon. Grinning broadly and not waiting to be invited, the other man pulled out a chair and sat down.

"Where's Mattie and the girls?" Cody asked.

"When I left them, they were headed for the Ferris wheel. I'd get on the back of Adam Harrison's bucking bronc before I'd climb on one of those contraptions."

Cody chuckled. He felt just about the same way.

"Katie sure is enjoying herself," Jon noted casually. "She's danced with just about every fellow in town. I think even young Jimmy Johnson got up the nerve to ask her."

"He did. Twice."

Jon arched a brow. "You keeping track?"

"Not much else to do while sitting here."

"You mean to tell me you haven't been able to charm some of the local ladies into taking a spin around the dance floor with you?"

Cody shrugged. "A few."

Jon frowned and studied his friend's profile. "Have you tried to charm Katie?"

Cody shook his head. "My brand of charm doesn't work well with your sister."

Jon laughed. "What did you do to upset her?"

"I offered her some free advice about her ex-husband earlier that she didn't appreciate." He reached up and absently rubbed his tender jaw. The lady had a dynamite right hook.

"Well, Gary isn't a real popular subject with her. I steer clear of it myself."

Cody turned his gaze to his friend. "You know he's still controlling her, don't you?"

Jon nodded. "Some. But she's making progress. You've got to give her credit for that."

"Maybe." Cody turned his attention back to the dance floor. The music had stopped and Kathleen was talking with Adam. She was gazing up at the other man as if he could reveal all the secrets of the universe.

"Give her some time, Cody," Jon suggested. "Fifteen years worth of influence doesn't disappear overnight."

"I suppose not," Cody murmured, his gaze still fastened on the couple across the way. When Adam bent and kissed her cheek, Cody felt every muscle in his body tense. A moment later Kathleen was turning away and starting across the floor alone. Cody settled back in the chair and tried to relax.

Kathleen made her way across the crowded dance floor, her mind made up. She couldn't deny having a wonderful time. It was fun dancing with the different guys and she especially enjoyed Adam's company. He was handsome and funny and charming and interesting. But he seemed to have one major flaw: He wasn't Cody.

At first she'd been irritated by her feelings. She didn't understand how Cody Washington had reached such a position in her life to overshadow everyone else in it. But he did and there didn't seem to be much she could do about it. Or maybe there wasn't much that she wanted to do about it.

She'd seen him dancing with other women and couldn't stop the sting of envy she'd felt when that slow smile of his had been bestowed upon another. It didn't make sense, but then not much else did either. Her entire life had been spent doing and being what everyone else wanted. If she was ever going to start reaching for what she wanted, she might as well start now with Cody. She didn't know where these feelings he stirred in her would lead, but she knew she had to find out. Right or wrong, she had to know.

She reached the edge of the platform just as the band struck up a slow ballad. She stopped directly in front of Cody and looked down into his closed features. Inwardly, she sighed. He wasn't an easy man, but he drew her as surely as a magnet draws steel.

"Would you care to dance, Mr. Washington?" she asked politely.

He considered her a long, unblinking moment before rising from the chair. He hoisted himself onto the edge of the stage and she caught his hand as he rose to his feet. She led him into the dancers and then turned into his arms. He held her loosely, but she lifted her arms upward and linked her fingers behind his neck. And then she laid her head against his shoulder, letting the music work its subtle magic.

She drew in the scent of him, clean and spicy. Beneath her ear she could hear his heart beating out a steady rhythm. She could feel him gradually relax. The stiffness seemed to leave him by degrees, until he was moving easily with her and the music. His hands traced lightly down her sides until they came to rest on the gentle curve of her hips. The now familiar heat was there between them, simmering.

When the song ended, Cody's hands tightened about her waist as if to push her away. She drew back to look up at him, but kept her arms linked behind his head. Her fingers began to tangle in the silky strands of hair there as he watched her with curious eyes.

As the band struck up a lively tune, she released him and backed away. She opened her mouth to speak at the same instant someone caught her arm. She turned to look up into Adam's warm eyes.

"How about another turn around the dance floor, darlin'."

She laughed lightly. "No thanks, Adam. I'm about danced out."

"Are you sure?" He reached for her hand.

"I'm sure." She pulled her hand free and turned back to Cody. She was stunned to find herself alone. There wasn't a sign of him as she scanned the crowd frantically.

She skirted the dance floor and paused at the edge to look out over the street crowded with milling people. Dusk was settling in, making it difficult to see in the half-light, but she finally spotted him making his way toward the parking area. She jumped down from the platform and hurried after him. He was at the truck, and she was out of breath when she finally caught up with him.

"Why did you leave like that?" she asked.

He pulled the truck door open and sailed his hat into the cab. Impatient fingers raked through his hair. "I thought you were done with me," he bit out.

"I wanted to talk to you. I was going to suggest that before Adam interrupted."

"I don't feel much like talking." He pulled his keys out of his jeans pocket. "I'm going home."

"You were just going to leave me," she accused.

"You can ride back on the bus."

"But I thought you were suppose to follow the bus in case there were problems."

"I'm sure the bus will be fine." He climbed into the cab and moved to pull the door closed, but she caught it with her hand.

"You're not leaving yet," she said, wedging her body between him and the door. "I want to talk to you."

He stared at her, speechless, for a long moment. Then suddenly he began to chuckle. He rested his head back against the seat and began to laugh in earnest.

Kathleen frowned. "What's so funny?" she asked defensively.

"This whole situation." He looked at her and shook his head. "Am I your guinea pig, Kathleen? What is it about me that makes you feel comfortable enough to want to test all of your new found assertive behavior techniques on me?"

She looked at him, calling herself every kind of fool for being hurt by his words. Tears clogged her throat, making a response impossible. She turned away and closed his door, determined not to embarrass herself further. Blinking furiously against the threatening moisture in her eyes, she started back toward town.

She'd taken less than ten steps when she heard Cody call her name. She managed only a few more steps before his hand closed around her arm.

"Come on," he said, tugging her back toward the truck. "We're going to straighten all this out now."

She walked beside him but didn't look at him. Hopefully the darkness would help conceal her feelings. If she could just gain control of the tears that threatened to overtake her. She felt like a big enough idiot already.

He led her to the rear of the truck and pulled the tailgate down. She gasped when his hands closed around her waist and he lifted her off the ground. "You sit," he ordered, as she found herself doing just that. Instantly she scrambled back to her feet.

"I don't want to sit," she announced firmly.

He glared at her and then sighed. "Fine. I'll sit." He perched on the edge of the tailgate. "Now what did you want to talk about?"

She shot him a quick glance, finding no encouragement in his posture. His arms were crossed against his chest and he looked like he'd like to be anywhere but here.

She drew in a deep breath and shook her head. "This is silly," she said quietly. "Go on home, Cody. You don't deserve this foolishness."

He didn't speak and didn't move. He just continued to watch her, his eyes curious, his expression intent. As uncomfortable as his steady gaze made her, Kathleen couldn't look away. She wondered what he saw when he studied her like that. Did he find anything appealing in her weak and uncertain character?

Her heart was beating in an uneven tempo as she closed the distance between them. Interest and caution sharpened his green eyes when she stopped directly in front of him. With trembling fingers, she lifted her hand to rest against the cheek she had struck that morning. He didn't flinch, but she felt him stiffen. She stroked him, enjoying the contrast between the soft skin and the overlying bristle of his beard.

"I'm sorry about this morning," she said softly. "I've never done anything like that before. I'm sorry it happened with you. You certainly don't deserve such treatment."

If she expected her apology to immediately set everything right between them, she was sadly mistaken. Not that she could really blame him. It did seem that she had been freely testing her aggressiveness on him. She'd challenged him at nearly every turn, always searching for a way to oppose him instead of stand with him. Now she wondered why. Why did he threaten her when he was by far the fairest man she'd ever known?

Deciding to risk her pride to the fullest, she let her hand slide around behind his neck and brought her other one up to join it. His initial resistance was felt as she applied a subtle pressure to bring his head down to hers. She looked into his brilliant eyes, moved by the uncertainty she saw there. Stretching upward, she let her eyes drift closed as her lips met his.

His response was cool, but she didn't give up. She let her lips warm his slowly as her fingers stroked along the taut muscles of his neck and shoulders. Patiently she whittled away at his reticence until finally, he groaned low in his throat and his hand came up to cup the back of her head.

She may have started the encounter, but he easily took control, dragging her into the center of whirling, blinding sensations. He slid forward on the tailgate until her body was nestled intimately to the firm lines of his own. His sudden heat seared her, and she melted against him as his mouth shifted and came back to deepen the kiss.

Her fingers curled into his shoulders as she responded with an abandon completely foreign to her. Never had she felt this kind of reckless yearning. The earth, the sky, the night all faded away into nothing as her senses centered solely on the man holding her. This madness was vivid and alive, and she willingly chased with him through the mindless swirl of emotion.

A loud explosion of sound overhead had her jerking away from him. Her eyes flew open to see an umbrella of sparkling blue and white light fill the black sky.

"Look what you've done now," Cody murmured low against her ear.

She looked back at him, mesmerized by the reflection of fading lights in his eyes. "I did that?" she asked breathlessly.

"Oh, yeah. Just by kissing me you've caused all these fireworks to go off."

At her puzzled frown he began to laugh. "Come on," he said, sliding back further into the truck bed and pulling her up with him. He leaned back against the side and settled her comfortably between his legs, her head pillowed on his chest, his hands resting lightly on her stomach. Kathleen relaxed against him, her own hands coming up to cover his.

As each shimmering display lit the night, Kathleen marveled at the beauty. But nothing could outshine the contentment she felt in the arms surrounding her.

Eight

"I can't believe I let you talk me into this," Kathleen puffed.

"You'll thank me later," Cody assured her. "There's nothing quite like a Montana sunrise."

She frowned, annoyed that she could barely breathe and he didn't even sound winded. He led the way along a well established path, his long stride easily eating up the distance. He didn't seem to notice that she was practically jogging to keep up with him. She was about to demand that he slow down when he veered off the path and into the woods.

She stopped. "Where are you going?"

"There's this perfect little spot up this way."

"Jon told me never to leave the path," she reminded him, glad for the chance to catch her breath.

Cody stopped and looked back at her. "We'll be okay. I know where I'm going." When she didn't immediately move to follow, he came back to her. "Trust me." With the simple request he stretched his hand toward her. And because he did, she slipped her hand into his.

They skirted through the trees, following a path that Cody obviously knew well even in the murky pre-dawn light. Kathleen was sure they were gradually climbing higher. Her breath grew shallow and her legs began to protest from the extra work. When she was positive she was going to collapse from sheer exertion, they stepped into a clearing and a totally different world.

"Oh," she sighed, the beauty stealing away what little breath she had left. A thick covering of pine needles cushioned her steps as she walked out into the middle of the clearing. Before her, a panoramic view of the mountains stretched endlessly. In the twilight, their outlines were mere shadows, blending together, undefined.

Cody led her to a flat, grass covered ledge jutting out of the side of the mountain. He tossed the blanket up, then climbed up and reached down for her. She took a few steps and peeked over the edge. It wasn't a sheer drop and probably would have been a piece of cake for an experienced mountain climber. But to her way of thinking, she didn't need to get any closer to realize they were quite a ways up.

She turned back to Cody and found him sitting comfortably on the blanket. "Have a seat," he invited, as he tossed his hat aside. "The show is about to start."

She dropped down beside him. "This is incredible," she whispered because it seemed somehow irreverent to speak aloud.

"You haven't seen anything yet." He scooted closer to her and pointed toward the mountains. "The sun will come up between those two peaks. It'll rise between them like a huge red ball floating up to the sky. You won't believe how breathtaking it is. And you won't believe how beautiful it is when the sunlight pushes the shadows back from the mountains."

Kathleen followed the direction of his finger and found the two peaks he was referring to. She drew her knees up and wrapped her arms around them. Anticipation and excitement mingled to skip along her nerve endings. The anticipation came in response to the beauty she'd been promised. The excitement came from the man beside her.

Her senses were once again humming. His scent wrapped itself around her, teasing her, instilling itself into her memory. He'd lifted his hand and brought it down to rest on her shoulder, his fingers lightly caressing. Was it his heart she heard pounding or her own?

The stillness surrounding them was profound, almost tangible. Nothing stirred in the trees or along the ground. The air was still, as if all of nature held its breath in anticipation of a new day.

Kathleen felt her own breath catch as the sky behind the mountains slowly, steadily lightened. Then a blush of red appeared between the mountain peaks Cody had indicated. Brush strokes of pink and orange and red drifted outward across the canvas of the sky. Shivers ran along her spine as the color deepened and the curvature of the rising sun became evident. Unwavering, it continued its ascent until, for a few brief moments, the red sphere was centered perfectly between two jagged peaks.

Sunlight glinted and sparkled and danced, its fingers eagerly pushing aside the gray canopy of night. As darkness receded, the mountains began to take shape, their peaks and valleys revealed as they challenged and overshadowed one another. As if on cue, nature joined the concert. It started with the cheerful song of one bird and grew in force until the forest was alive with the music of life. Kathleen was awed with the perfect orchestration of it all. Never again would she take a sunrise for granted.

"Was it worth the walk?"

"Yes." She turned to Cody and saw him frown.

He lifted a hand to her cheek. "You're crying."

She hadn't known she was, but it didn't surprise her. Beauty, in any capacity, had the power to move her.

She felt his fingers slide into her hair and cup the back of her head. She saw the intention in his eyes before she felt the slight pressure he applied to draw her to him. There was no resistance in her. She lifted her hands to his shoulders, wanting to feel the solid strength beneath the soft cotton of his shirt. Her eyes drifted shut just as his lips found hers. The kiss was as gentle as the morning, as breathtaking as the sunrise. Desire sparked through her, dancing from his body to hers and threatening to outshine the sunlight pouring down on them.

His lips left hers and began a leisurely exploration along her cheek to her neck. Automatically, she tilted her head back, giving him full access to the sensitive area. His lips worked magic, easily transporting her into a world ruled by heightened sensation. Her senses were flooded with him and nature and an ever growing passion.

Cody couldn't recall ever tasting anything as sweet as her skin. At the base of her throat he felt her pulse flutter against his lips. He teased it with his tongue and felt the tempo increase. His hands skimmed down her back until they came to rest at her waist. She was wearing a heavy red sweater with fat wooden buttons down the front. The material was soft beneath his palms, but it wasn't enough. He wanted to feel the ripple of bare skin beneath his touch. Easily, his hands tunneled under the hem of the sweater, instantly granting him the pleasure of her warm flesh.

Kathleen jerked, his touch coming as a bold surprise. She waited and anticipated as his hands slowly trailed upwards over her ribs until they encountered the silky material of her bra. With his lips still nuzzling her neck, he inserted the tip of one finger beneath the barrier and traced the edge toward the front. She gasped and his mouth was there to swallow the sound. Her fingers dug into his shoulders as his kiss swept her away on a surging wave of desire and need.

As many times as she had questioned her ability to arouse a man, she couldn't do so now. Cody wanted her. It was a fact she knew on some intricate feminine level. It was a fact that exhilarated her and heightened her own response. She had never experienced desire this intense. But then, it seemed that everything she experienced with this man was intense.

Cody moaned as her body arched closer to his own and her fingers curled into his shoulders. He was no stranger to desire, but nothing had ever sent him soaring as high and fast as this woman did. Her ex-husband must have been a blind fool not to see the powder keg of passion she possessed. Well, Cody was nobody's fool. He knew if he didn't put a stop to the fire he and Kathleen were playing with, they were bound to blow a hole in the side of this mountain.

Drawing on his badly battered restraint, he tore his mouth away from hers. She moaned softly and lifted her hands to frame his face.

Fervently her lips began to roam his features. He felt his control slip another notch before trying to ease her away. But she was having none of it. She twisted around until she was able to push him down onto the blanket. His weak resistance was completely shattered when her mouth teased his with a boldness he couldn't ignore. With a groan of absolute surrender, he wrapped his arms around her waist and laid back on the blanket, taking her with him.

Kathleen had never experienced this kind of sensual power. It was as if years of unfulfilled desire had come together to be expressed here with this man, in this place. With her body covering his, there was no denying the need she aroused in him. She heard his groan of pleasure and knew she was the cause. She felt his body shudder and knew it was for her alone. He was hers and nothing else mattered.

She pushed upward until she was sitting astride his hips. With quick movements she released the buttons of his shirt and pulled the tails out of his jeans. She parted the material and let her hands glide through the curling hair on his chest. His flesh was warm and his chest was heaving as he strained to draw in air. When she let her hand drift downward over his taut stomach, she was sure he'd stopped breathing altogether. But when she looked up into his face she found herself under the sharp scrutiny of flaring green eyes. And in that one telling look she realized her control would only last as long as he let it.

She shot him a wicked smile and eased her hands upward again. Her fingers grazed his nipples and she heard and felt his sharp intake of breath. Intrigued, she let her fingers tease the sensitive areas again and was rewarded by his response. His eyes closed as a low moan tore through him.

Seconds later his fingers flew up and closed around her wrists, pulling her hands away. "Enough," he ground out.

"Yeah, you look like you're suffering," she teased. She drew her hands from his grip and reached up to release the buttons running down the front of her sweater.

Mesmerized, Cody watched her fingers. When the last button was freed, she slipped the garment down her arms and tossed it aside. She reached behind her back and a second later the bra joined the sweater.

His mouth went dry as the air backed up in his lungs. With the

morning sun glinting off her porcelain skin and sparkling through
her blond curls, she looked like some kind of erotic angel. Automatically, his hands reached up to cup her breasts, eliciting a sigh
of pleasure from her.

Kathleen was sure she'd never felt anything so glorious. All of
her inhibitions seemed to float away like a helium filled balloon.
She felt as free as that balloon, as if she and Cody were at the edge
of the universe, alone and destined for nothing more than pleasing
one another. The sun warming her skin was a potent aphrodisiac
surpassed only by the feel of Cody's teasing touch. Never had she
experienced this all-consuming need that spread rapidly through
her body. Never had she expected to.

When the potent sensations became nearly more than she could
bear, she leaned forward, nestling fully against his body. Her arms
wound around his neck, and she looked down into his eyes. "I
want to make love with you," she whispered.

His hands stroked up and down her back as his common sense
battled his libido. Making love to her was not a unique idea. He
couldn't deny that he'd entertained the thought on more than one
occasion. It was just that he'd envisioned it happening in a more
traditional location. He had wanted it to be perfect for her. He'd
wanted to tenderly share with her the joys of mutual loving. But
she seemed to be finding out a few things on her own. And there
was plenty to be said for the surrounding solitude of nature and
the sunshine warming their skin.

When he didn't immediately respond, she dipped her head and
began to nibble gently at his bottom lip. It took less than a half
dozen heartbeats to pull him back under her spell. When she moved
her hips suggestively against his own, he gave himself up as lost.
If she was determined to seduce him, then so be it. A man could
face a worse fate.

She drove him to the edge of sanity in record time. She experi-
mented with her newfound powers and he reaped the benefits. She
teased and tempted and promised, and he fought the blatant urge
to take control from her and bring an end to the erotic play. The
feel of her hands and mouth moving over his body held him captive;
a willing prisoner.

When she stretched out above him and his hands were able to
move in one smooth unbroken path from her shoulders to her hips,

he was startled into a moment of clear thinking. He had no memory of how the remainder of their clothing had disappeared, but there was no denying the fact that they were flesh to flesh now.

"Katie. . . ." he murmured against her neck. Her lips were burning a trail of moist kisses along his collarbone and he struggled to retain his original thought. He knew it was important. If he could think clearly for half a second he was sure he'd remember.

She lifted her head and looked down into his face with blue eyes dazed by passion. A smile curved her lips. "I'm going to love you like no one ever has," she promised.

His hand trembled as it came up to cup her cheek. "You already have." He ran his thumb along her swollen lips. Abruptly, he remembered what had been so important a moment ago. "I've got something to protect you in my wallet."

She shook her head, a shadow from the past moving briefly through her eyes. "There's no need," she whispered. "I'm permanently protected."

He started to question her, but she shifted slightly, and he was unable to do anything but respond. He arched upward and they came together in what seemed to be a perfect fit. When she began to move, he was completely at her mercy. His mind closed down to everything but the sensations pouring through his body. But he was certain as he made the ascent toward fulfillment that she was flying right there beside him.

Cody felt her tears on his chest and tightened his arms around her. His heartbeat was still racing and tremors still racked her body. Incredible. The adjective did not aptly describe what he'd just experienced, but it was as close as he could come at the moment. He looked up into a cloudless blue sky and realized that his life had just taken a major and unexpected detour. He was amazed to realize it wasn't one that disappointed him.

He shifted their positions until she was lying on her back and he was looking down into her tear stained face. He reached out and gently wiped the moisture away; then bent and placed a gentle kiss against her lips.

He drew away and shook his head. "You are one fantastic lady. I have never experienced anything like that in all my life." He saw the uncertainty in her eyes and felt a quick stab of anger. "I've never lied to you, Katie," he said evenly. "I'm not going to start now."

She reached up and touched his cheek. "I know," she murmured. "Thank you for letting me set the pace. I guess I was using you as my guinea pig again."

He grinned. "Anytime, sweetheart. Just let me know, and I'll be there."

She wound her arms around his neck and hugged him tight. "God, Cody, it was fantastic," she said against his skin. "I never knew it could feel like that."

"I told you it was never your fault. There's nothing wrong with you, Kathleen. There never has been."

She drew back to look at him. "Now that I know what I've been missing all these years I may be tempted to make up for lost time." She smiled softly. "I don't suppose you'd like to volunteer to help me with that?"

"Lady, I think I could probably match you every step of the way."

"Do you?" She narrowed her eyes and ran a hand downward over his chest and stomach. His body responded without hesitation to her light touch. She was impressed. He was downright amazed. He couldn't recall the last time a woman had aroused him as easily as Kathleen did. He couldn't recall the last time he'd wanted a woman as badly as he did Kathleen. She stirred a magnitude of emotions in him. One of these days he was going to have to sit down and try to sort through all of those emotions. One of these days, but not now. Now he had other things to think about.

"Now look what you've gone and done," he said, as he pressed her back against the blanket. "You can't leave a man like this, you know."

Her eyes widened with mock innocence. "You can't?" she asked breathlessly. "I guess you'll have to do whatever is necessary to remedy the situation."

"I guess I will," he replied smoothly as he prepared to show her this particular ride seldom felt the same way twice.

When Cody jumped down from the ledge and reached up to lift Kathleen down, the sun was high in the morning sky. She slipped her hand in his as they started to leave the area, but she held back a moment just before they stepped into the woods.

He watched her as she ran her gaze over the little piece of heaven. "Can we come back sometime?" she asked, turning to him.

He smiled and marveled at the fact that he wanted her again. She looked like a woman who had been well-loved. He should probably remind her to restore some order to her hair. He doubted that her lips would lose much of their swollen fullness by the time they arrived back at the ranch. It didn't matter. He liked leaving his stamp on her. Hell, if he had a mirror to look in, he'd probably discover that he looked just as sated as she did.

"We'll come back," he promised her. "Often."

She laughed as he turned and started the trip back. It was easier going down than it had been coming up. Of course, she didn't think Cody was moving as fast as he had earlier. A purely feminine smile curved her lips as she wondered if he was just a little tired. She couldn't remember the last time she'd felt the boundless energy she did now. Actually, she didn't think she'd ever felt this good. It must be true what they said about good sex.

Mentally, she stumbled on that thought. Was it just sex? Could she experience what she had this morning in Cody's arms with another man? Say Adam maybe? She thought about it only a moment before she had her answer—a resounding no. Just as Gary had never been able to stir any fires in her soul, neither would Adam.

There was something more between her and Cody that made their coming together so perfect. Despite their earlier clashes, she knew that she cared for him. He made her feel special. He must care for her. She didn't think he would have let this morning happen if he didn't. He seemed to be a man who was comfortable with the life he'd made for himself. Surely he wouldn't have become involved with her unless he was comfortable with that, too.

Just how involved were they now? She turned the question over in her mind carefully. She'd just ended a fifteen year relationship that had nearly destroyed her. She was not looking to establish another one. Cody was thirty-eight and obviously settled in his single lifestyle. He didn't appear to be looking to establish any kind of long-term relationship. So where did that leave them? As lovers? She nearly cringed at the word.

"So have you figured it out yet?" His question sliced into her uneasy thoughts.

They had just emerged from the woods to follow the well-defined path. She shot him a quick glance. "What?" she asked innocently.

"Whatever it is that has you so concerned," he returned smoothly. "I can see you trying to organize it all in your mind."

She shrugged. "I'm just thinking about some things."

He slid her a glance, his brow arched. "Mind if I offer you some free advice?"

"Okay."

"Don't try to put any labels on what you're feeling right now. And definitely don't try to put any labels on me. Chances are none of them will fit a month from now."

Silently she mulled over his words. Was he trying to tell her that the tenuous relationship between them now would be over within a few weeks? Maybe he knew that because it was a pattern he was used to following. Maybe he knew what was between them would never grow because he would never allow it to. And that was okay, wasn't it? She didn't really want anything lasting from him. Did she?

"Kathleen?"

She jerked her gaze up to meet his. They had stopped walking, and he was watching her with sharp green eyes. In the distance she could hear sounds from the ranch. He released her hand and lifted his to brush his fingertips across her cheek. A moment later, he bent and dropped a soft, lingering kiss on her lips. Her heart was pounding at an unreasonable tempo after just that brief caress.

He smiled. "Fix your hair," he said quietly. "It looks like a man has been running his fingers through it."

Instantly her hands flew upward and she began to comb her fingers through the tossed curls. He watched her and then nodded when a semblance of order had been restored.

"Maybe you better consider wearing your hat anytime we're going to be together," he suggested. "It's a great way to cover up one tell-tale sign." He shook his head as a definite sparkle of mischief lit his eyes. "Too bad we can't do anything about your swollen lips, though."

Her fingers lifted to her mouth as he turned away. Her lips were tender beneath her touch, and she could only imagine how they looked. Cody had started on ahead of her and she stood a moment and watched with undisguised admiration. She knew now what was concealed beneath those jeans and shirt. Desire sparked deep in her stomach at the memory. Suddenly it occurred to her that getting over Cody Washington might not be an easy thing to do.

He turned then and looked at her. "Come on," he called. "They're probably about ready to send a search party out after us."

She started after him, wondering for the first time if the morning would turn out to be an irrevocable mistake.

"Heather, you know I'm not doing this just to upset you." Kathleen tried to reason, knowing it was falling on deaf ears.

The girl glowered at her from where she was perched on the edge of the sofa beside Holly. "I told you I didn't want to stay here," she cried. "Why are you doing this to us?"

"I told you that I like it here. . . ."

"But what about us?" Heather insisted. "You keep talking about you. When did you stop to think about us?"

"I am thinking about you. I have to be able to provide for you and Holly. Mr. Washington has made me a job offer that I'd be foolish to pass up."

"What's so special about it? Why couldn't you get the same kind of job in Chicago? You worked in the museum there. Why can't you go back to it?"

"They didn't pay me, Heather. It was volunteer work."

"I don't care!" Heather jumped up and whirled away. "We've done okay so far without you working. Daddy's taking care of us."

Kathleen let out a frustrated breath and leaned back against Jon's desk. Well, she couldn't say that she was surprised by her daughter's reaction. So far it had been nothing less than she'd expected.

"I don't want your father to support me," she explained patiently. "It's important that I'm able to support myself and you girls."

Heather turned to her, her blue eyes swimming with tears. "Mom, why can't we go home?" she asked, her voice wavering. "I know if you went back and talked to Daddy you could work everything out. I know we could be a family again."

Kathleen shook her head. "Honey, that's not ever going to happen. Daddy and I are never going to get back together. You've got to give up that idea."

"Why?" Heather demanded, tears sliding down her cheeks. "I know if you went back and talked to him he'd take you back. I'm sure he'd forgive you if. . . ."

"Heather." Kathleen grasped the trembling girl by the shoulders and gave her a quick shake. Heather, startled by the unfamiliar strength in her mother's voice and action, stared up at her. "It's time you understood some things," Kathleen said firmly. "I do not want to go back to your father. I don't need or want his forgiveness. That part of my life is over now."

"But how can you throw it away so easily? Don't all those years mean something to you?"

Kathleen shook her head. "Not anymore," she said bleakly. "It's over, honey. You need to accept that."

Heather jerked away and rushed to the door. "I hate it here, and I'm not staying," she stated emphatically. "I'll call Daddy and he'll let me live with him." With her intentions firmly stated, she pulled the door open and fled from the room.

Kathleen stared at the empty doorway and lifted a hand to rub her forehead. She didn't know whether to scream or cry or just kick something. There was no reasoning with her headstrong daughter. And she didn't even want to think about the upcoming crisis she'd face when Gary told Heather she couldn't live with him.

"Mom?"

Kathleen turned, remembering that Holly was still there. "I'm sorry, honey," she said ruefully. "I think your opinion got lost in the explosion."

Holly stood and smiled. "I'm used to it."

Kathleen opened her arms and Holly walked into them to share a hug. Kathleen stroked the silky blond hair and silently thanked God that she didn't have to deal with two rebellious teenagers right now.

"I'll go talk to Heather," Holly offered as she drew away. "Maybe she'll listen to me."

"Thanks." Kathleen touched her cheek and frowned slightly. "What about you, honey? Are you okay with this decision?"

"I love it," Holly assured her. "I'm excited about living here. Do you think Uncle Jon will still let me work on the ranch after we move?"

"I'm sure he will. We'll talk to him."

"Good." Holly smiled. "I better go find Heather." She walked to the door and paused there a moment, her gaze going back to her mother. "Daddy won't let her live with him will he."

Kathleen recognized the fact that Holly wasn't asking a question. She was stating the situation as she saw it. And as always, Holly's instincts were a hundred percent correct when it came to pegging her father.

"I don't think so," Kathleen said sadly. "I'm afraid Heather's going to be very disappointed."

"She'll be hurt." The girl frowned. "Why can't she see how he really is?"

Kathleen hesitated and drew a deep breath. "I guess she's convinced herself he's the way she wants him to be." She shrugged helplessly. "I can't explain it, and I don't know if she'll ever see his true colors."

"Do you think he loves us at all?"

Kathleen's heart cracked a little more. Holly had always been the more reticent of the two girls. She observed everything closely and carefully and based her opinions on those observations. Her maturity and natural common sense had awed Kathleen on more than one occasion. It was as if she had been born wise. Sometimes Kathleen wished she'd been a little less astute.

"I think he loves you as much as he can," Kathleen said flatly.

Holly silently digested her words and then nodded as if accepting them as the truth. "I'll go and find Heather," she said before disappearing out the door.

Nine

Kathleen sighed and walked to the window looking out over the back of the ranch. From here she could see the horses grazing in the paddock. Off in the distance she could see one of the cowboys repairing a section of fence. And further off she could just make out a group of riders starting out on one of the many trails that crisscrossed the ranch.

It had rained last night, washing away the dust and leaving the new day brighter and fresher. It was such a vivid world out here in this modern day wilderness. If someone would have told her a year ago that she would one day want to live here, she would have laughed at them. She'd grown up in Chicago, and had fully expected to spend her entire life there. Unlike Jon, she hadn't been born with the love of this wild land mysteriously ingrained in her heart. She'd had to see it before she fell in love. Somehow all this vast open space soothed her. She was at peace here.

"A penny for your thoughts."

She jumped as the deep voice came close to her ear and two hands settled firmly onto her shoulders.

"Sorry," Cody offered as he bent and dropped a warm kiss against her neck. "I didn't realize you were so deep in thought."

She sighed and closed her eyes. Without conscious thought she leaned back against his hard frame. "I was just thinking how much I love it here."

He wrapped his arms around her and rested his cheek against her hair. "Well, I can think of at least one person who is very happy to hear that."

She smiled and let herself enjoy his embrace. These tender moments with him she wouldn't trade for anything in the world. Her feelings for him grew with each passing day, but she refused to get lost in the maze of trying to define them. For now it was enough just to spend a little of each day with him. She enjoyed his company, enjoyed the way he made her feel. It was enough. For now.

"Rumor has it," he murmured, "that you've decided to make Montana your permanent home."

"No rumor. It's a fact. I accepted your dad's job offer this morning."

"I saw the girls out at the stables. You must have just told them. I got the impression one of them isn't very happy about your decision."

Kathleen sighed. "No. I'm afraid one of them is very upset right now."

"What about Holly? Is she okay with the plan?"

"She's fine. But Heather is dead set against it, and I don't know what to do about it."

"Maybe it's time daddy stepped in and got involved."

Kathleen gave a humorless chuckle. "It's way past time for

daddy to get involved. Unfortunately, daddy doesn't want to be involved."

"She told me she's going back to Chicago to live with him. Is that true?"

Kathleen turned in his arms to face him. "Heather wants to believe that. But I can't imagine Gary ever agreeing to that. It would inconvenience him."

Cody reached up and threaded his fingers through her hair. "I've never met this man and I don't like him much."

"Gary is very selfish and self-centered. I've known that all along. But something's been nagging at me the last few days." She looked up into Cody's face, enjoying the warmth in his eyes and the feel of his hands lightly caressing her back. "Maybe he would have been different with another woman. Maybe he's different with Jackie, the woman he's living with now. Maybe I was the reason. . . ."

"Kathleen, don't," Cody ordered tersely.

"No, just listen a minute." She laid a hand on his chest. "I didn't know how exciting making love could be until I was with you. I never responded to Gary like I did you the other morning. Maybe it's the same thing with him. Maybe he's not as selfish with Jackie. Maybe Gary and I just brought out the worst in each other."

Cody stared down at her, doubt clearly marking his features. "I think you're too easy on the guy," he said bluntly. "I think you're still looking for ways to excuse his inexcusable behavior."

She lowered her gaze and tried to turn away, but he held her tight. "The truth of the matter is, Kathleen, I don't give a damn about your ex-husband except for the fact that he's hurting your daughters and leaving you to clean up the mess. I'll be perfectly happy if he never sets foot in Montana." His hand moved around to cup the back of her head. "You're here with me now and that's all I care about."

Pleasure bloomed deep inside her as a smile curved her lips. The possessive note in his voice should have annoyed her, but it didn't. The idea of belonging to Cody Washington had a very appealing ring to it. She tilted her head to the side. "Are you staking your claim?" she asked playfully.

"Oh, yeah," he breathed as he bent toward her. "I'm staking it strong and deep." His mouth closed over hers without any kind of gentle prelude. Hot and insistent, he took what he wanted and then some. Her arms slid around his neck as he crushed her body to the length of his. She held on and made her own demands.

"Oh, my gosh! I'm sorry." A loud thump had Cody and Kathleen springing apart. Mattie was kneeling on the floor, frantically trying to retrieve the mail that had scattered in twelve different directions.

"I hope that package wasn't breakable," Cody remarked as he walked over to her.

"It's just books," she assured him. "I didn't know anyone was in here."

"Well, that's understandable," he said easily as he crouched down beside her. "Kathleen had been talking but I was doing my best to keep her quiet."

Mattie rose and carried the armload of mail to the desk. She piled it there and turned back to the couple across the room. A mischievous smile curved her lips. "I really am sorry I interrupted. I'll leave now, if you'd like."

"No," Cody said, "I think I better be going." He looked at Kathleen. "Actually, I did have a legitimate reason for being here. I wanted to ask you when you wanted to start work on the museum."

"I don't know. I didn't talk to Olan about any of that."

"You don't need to talk to him. You need to talk to me." He grinned wickedly. "I'm your cheap labor."

Mattie laughed outright. "Oh, you're real cheap all right."

He sent her a dark look. "No comments from the spectators." He turned his attention back to Kathleen. "I can purchase all the paint and supplies. We can start next week if you want."

She nodded. "Sounds good to me."

He extended his hand. "Partners?"

She smiled and gripped his hand. "Partners."

Cody paused in his work to enjoy the enticing view from his vantage point. Kathleen was across the room perched half way up on a ladder, her back to him. With careful strokes she applied antique white paint to the wall with a roller. He grinned, noticing that at some point she must have stuck her hand in the paint. An almost perfect imprint of her hand was smeared across the backside of her jeans. He thought he wouldn't mind leaving his hand print there, too.

"What do you say we call it quits after we finish this room," he suggested.

She paused and looked at him over her shoulder. "Are you tired?"

He gave a short laugh. "Hell, lady, you're a slave driver. You've worked me almost twelve hours a day for the last four. It's Friday night. Give me a break."

She arched a brow. "Do you have a date?" she inquired mildly.

"Maybe," he returned in the same tone of voice. "I haven't asked her yet."

She turned her back to him and went back to work. "You're taking a pretty big chance aren't you?"

"God, I hope so." He crossed the room and caught her around the waist. She squealed as he pulled her down into his arms. His lips claimed hers before she could begin to scold him. With a sigh, she settled into the kiss, letting her arms rest on his shoulders. He lowered his hands to her hips and told himself he was just checking to see if the paint there was still wet.

"At this rate I suppose we could hope for a Christmas opening."

Cody swore under his breath as he drew away from Kathleen. He looked over her shoulder to see his father standing in the doorway. "Hello, Dad," he greeted calmly.

"Hello, Cody." His green eyes sparkled with amusement as he lowered his gaze. "Nice paint job," he commented dryly.

Cody grinned and dropped his hands. Kathleen turned to Olan thinking he was referring to the paint on the walls. "Does it look okay?" she asked anxiously.

He chuckled softly. "It looks great," he assured her.

Cody cleared his throat and turned away. "We were about to call it a day," he said. "Would you like a tour?"

Olan slipped his hands into the pockets of his gray dress pants. "Not really," he said with a shrug. "I was just on my way into Bozeman and thought I'd stop by to see how things were coming. I can see you're making progress."

Kathleen set her roller aside and wiped her hands on a towel she had sticking out of the waist of her jeans. "What do you think about a mid-September opening?" she asked. "That gives me almost two full months to get everything in order."

"I'm not on any time schedule," Olan assured her. "Take your time and do things the way you want. When you can target a date to open, let me know and I'll have Jenny send out the invitations and announcements."

Kathleen nodded her agreement.

Cody was watching his father with interest. He hadn't come any further into the room, seeming content to hover just inside the doorway. To Cody's knowledge, this was the first time Olan had set foot in the place since his mother's death. It was painfully obvious that this first step was not an easy one for him.

"Well, I'm going to go on," Olan said. "I just thought I'd stop and see how things are coming. It looks great what you've done."

"We're coming along okay," Cody agreed.

Olan nodded and then turned toward the door. "See you two later." A few moments passed before the sound of his car engine starting drifted through the open windows.

Kathleen frowned and looked up at Cody. "Do you think he'll be able to come in here when it's finished?" she asked, concern shining in her eyes.

Cody shrugged. "I don't know," he said honestly. "At least he's trying. Maybe it'll get easier each time he tries."

"I hope so. He looked so uncomfortable."

"He was," Cody said thoughtfully. They stood a moment longer in a pensive silence until he mentally shrugged it off. He swung his gaze to her. "Now where were we before we were so rudely interrupted?"

She pushed his hand away as he reached for her. "We were painting," she said firmly. "Your suggestion to quit early sounds like a good idea. Let's finish up here and call it a day."

"All right. Will you go out to Dillon's with me later?"

She smiled. "Sure."

"Will you dance all the slow ones with me?" he asked silkily.

"Every single one," she purred.

He groaned deep in his throat, encouraged by the promise. Leaning over, he dropped a quick kiss on her lips. When he turned away, he began to whistle a cheery tune.

The live band was turning out a decent rendition of a classic Eagle's song. Kathleen rested her head against Cody's chest and let herself drift with the music and the man. It was amazing how completely her opinion of him had changed in a few short weeks. She remembered how she'd wanted to avoid him when she'd come here the first time. Now, she didn't think she could get close enough to him.

His lips brushed her temple. "Why do I get the impression you're about to fall asleep on me?" he asked close to her ear.

She smiled and drew back. "I find being this close to you very soothing."

His brow shot upward. "Then I'd better come up with something to shake you up," he decided. "Soothing you is not at all what I had in mind."

"Oh? Just what did you have in mind? I only agreed to dancing."

His eyes narrowed as he studied her. "There are a lot of different ways to dance," he told her, his voice husky.

She felt a shiver of response trail down her spine. All it took was a smokey look and a suggestive comment issued in that smokey voice to send her pulse into overdrive. The song ended and she stepped out of his arms. "Why don't we talk about it over another drink," she suggested.

His hand rested warmly on her waist as he followed her back to their table. He took a moment to admire the sway of her hips beneath her black skirt and the nylon covered length of her legs. There wasn't even a shadow of the frail woman who had arrived in Montana a few short weeks ago. She had been transformed into this incredibly lovely lady by his side. He knew he wasn't alone in his assessment of her. All evening long she had been receiving admiring glances from a fair share of the male patrons present. She gave no indication of noticing. But Cody had sent out a subtle message of his own: The lady is taken—back off.

He caught the waitress's attention and ordered two more drinks before he pulled his chair out and settled across from Kathleen at the small table. Reaching across, he captured her hand and threaded his fingers with hers.

"Can I tell you how beautiful you look tonight?" he asked.

She quickly averted her gaze, and he gave her hand a quick squeeze. "Don't do that," he ordered. Her eyes instantly lifted to his, but he could see that she was still uncomfortable with the praise. He sighed and lifted her hand to his lips for a light kiss.

"Why is it so difficult for you to accept a compliment?" he asked as he lowered their hands to the table.

"I guess because I haven't received a whole lot of them in the past," she answered honestly.

"Do you suppose if I keep dishing them out, that you'll eventually grow used to hearing them?"

"I hope I don't ever get used to you saying nice things to me."

It was moments like this that he was reminded of how very innocent she really was. He tended to forget that all of this was new to her. Actually, he suspected that he intentionally pushed that knowledge out of his mind. He didn't want to feel like he was taking unfair advantage of her. He didn't want to feel it even when he knew it was true.

She had just gained her freedom, was just learning to test her wings. It was unnerving to realize that he could very well be a stepping stone on her journey to a new life. He wanted to believe that he would never hold her back. He wanted to believe that he would never prevent her from testing those wings fully if she chose to. He wanted to believe it, but as each day passed he became less sure of himself.

What he felt for this woman surpassed anything he had experienced before. He found himself in unfamiliar territory, made even more complicated by her circumstances. Never had he been tempted to try to picture a future that included one woman. He found the idea easy enough to picture when that woman was Kathleen. That thought alone was enough to terrify him.

"Earth to Cody. Earth to Cody."

His attention snapped back to the present to find Kathleen slowly moving her hand in front of his face. Her smile was curious when she realized his eyes were actually focused on her. "You slipped away there for a few minutes, didn't you," she said with a bemused laugh. "You're hard on my fragile ego."

"Sorry. I guess I took a little side trip."

The waitress quickly placed their drinks in front of them before hurrying off. Kathleen let her gaze wander around the room as she sipped her drink. The evening was still young and already the place was packed. She recognized a few cowboys from the ranch and saw that some of the guests had stopped in to experience the local nightlife.

She turned back to Cody and studied him a moment. "Are you aware that you attract a lot of female attention?" she asked frankly.

He shook his head and tried to keep a straight face. "I hadn't noticed."

"It's true. I've been noticing it all evening. There's a brunette over there at the bar that's been trying to get close to you since she walked in here forty-five minutes ago."

Automatically he turned his head to scan the women at the bar. Sure enough, a shapely brunette with long legs and a lot of cleavage gave him an encouraging smile and an open invitation. He turned back to meet Kathleen's piercing gaze. "Imagine that," he said solemnly.

She took a long swallow of her drink. "Of course I can't blame her or any of the others," she said casually. "The way you fill out those jeans and that shirt would draw any woman's attention."

Cody blinked and then reached for her glass. "How many of these have you had?" he asked, humor lacing his words.

"That's only my second."

"It's only your last," he stated. "I think the liquor is loosening your tongue and heightening your imagination."

She shook her head adamantly. "No, it's not. I know what I'm seeing. Besides a woman feels these things, too. You can't deny that the brunette is coming on to you."

"Sure she is," he admitted easily. "But the cowboy three tables over has been trying to work up the nerve for the last hour to ask you to dance."

Kathleen laughed and didn't even bother to try to search out her would-be admirer. It would have been ridiculous for her to have done so. Men did not, had never, picked her out of a crowd. Especially when there was a buxom brunette on the premises.

"You don't believe me, do you," Cody said softly. "You think I'm making it all up."

"I think it's sweet of you to do so."

"Damn it, Kathleen!"

She jumped, his anger catching her off guard. She stared at him as he pushed his chair back and stood. "Let's go," he ordered brusquely as he tossed a few bills onto the table.

She stood and his hand took up its proprietary presence on her elbow as they maneuvered toward the door. Every step of the way her temper gathered force. By the time they stepped out into the cool night, she was steaming full force. She immediately jerked her arm away and rounded on him.

"Don't you ever do that to me again," she hissed. Before he could respond, she whirled away and hurried toward his truck.

"Do what?" he demanded when he caught up with her.

"Order me around like you own me or something."

"Wait a minute." He caught her arm, drawing her to an abrupt halt.

"No, you wait a minute." She pulled her arm free again and pushed at his chest. "Just because we've slept together don't go thinking that you can treat me like some cheap piece that you've picked up and paid for."

He muttered a curse that left her momentarily speechless. His fingers bit into her arms and he hauled her close. "When have I ever treated you with anything less than the respect you deserve?" he ground out. "When, Kathleen?" He released her sharply and swung away.

She stood a moment and absently rubbed her arms where the bite of his fingers could still be felt. She watched as his long stride carried him swiftly to his truck. Once there, he didn't get inside, but disappeared into the shadows. She drew in an unsteady breath and moved to follow him at a slower pace.

She found him leaning against the vehicle, his elbows resting on the edge of the bed. "I'm sorry," she said quietly. "I was out of line back there."

He gave a sharp laugh and dropped his head. He stood that way for a long time and she waited. When he finally spoke, she had to strain to hear his words. "You make me crazy, Kathleen. How could you believe that I would ever think less of you because we'd made love?"

"I. . . . I don't know," she stuttered. "I didn't really. I was just lashing out at you." She hesitated. "Why did you get angry with me in there?"

He blew out a deep breath and turned to gaze at her. "Why do you find it so hard to believe that men can find you attractive?" he countered.

"Because they never have."

"Is that a fact?" he challenged. "Do I even have to ask who's fed you that bull?"

Her silence was profound. He turned away and reached up to rub his forehead. "I'm so damned tired of running into his shadow every time I turn around," he said wearily. "When are you going to turn him loose, Kathleen? When are you going to stop listening to and believing everything he's ever told you?"

He didn't wait for a response from her. He pushed away from the truck and reached over to open the passenger door. "Can we go now?" he asked stiffly.

Silently, Kathleen climbed into the truck. She didn't know what she could say to him. There didn't seem to be anything at all to say.

The drive back to the ranch was accomplished in total silence. Kathleen was struggling with a multitude of uncertain feelings. She regretted that she had hurt him with her hasty accusations. Since it was impossible to take the words back, she'd done the next best thing and apologized. But she knew it wasn't enough. He wanted something from her she couldn't give him. At least not yet. It was not an easy matter to alter the mindset she'd lived with for the last fifteen years. She'd be the first to admit that Gary's influence was still hovering over her. But, as much as she would like, she couldn't change everything overnight. She needed time. Lots of it.

As they neared the point where the gravel road split, Cody slowed the truck to a stop. Kathleen frowned and looked over at him. He was staring out the windshield as if uncertain of which road to choose. Finally he turned his head to meet her gaze. In the shadowy confines of the truck cab they stared at one another.

She felt the unvoiced question between them and wasn't sure if he was asking her or himself. Without thinking, she reached out and drew his hand to her lips. She placed a gentle kiss to his palm, hearing his softly indrawn breath. "Make love to me tonight," she requested simply.

She felt his fingers close around hers briefly before he withdrew his hand. He shifted the truck into gear and turned his attention back to the road. Ten minutes later he was parking next to the small cabin he called home.

It was almost like existing inside a dream. He led her to the door of the cabin and inside. He didn't bother with lights, but moved with assurance through the dark.

Kathleen had no concept of where she was. It was a strangely erotic sensation. Everything was concealed by thick shadows, including the man who had turned to her and tenderly framed her face with his hands. His lips found hers and began a teasing game that had her straining for solid contact.

As if to make up for her lack of vision, her other senses kicked into high gear. His familiar scent came to her wrapped in a seductive whisper. She lifted her hands and let her fingertips stroke restlessly across the solid muscle of his shoulders until they delved into the silky hair at his nape.

As he continued to torment her with short butterfly kisses, his hands left her face and traced slowly downward over her body until his fingers found the buttons trailing down the front of her blouse. He freed each one easily and then slipped the garment off her shoulders. She heard it fall to the floor with a soft rustle at the same instant his mouth covered hers fully. She moaned as mindless pleasure shot through her. Her lips parted under his in a blatant invitation that he chose to ignore in favor of sampling the tempting flesh beneath her ear and along the column of her neck.

Sweet frustration had her sighing his name and her fingers tensing in his hair, but he didn't alter his course. She tilted her head granting him unobstructed access. With deliberate care he ran moist kisses along her collarbone. Her breath died in her lungs as sure fingers played lazily along her spine. A heartbeat later her bra was disposed of. The world took a crazy spin when his warm hands cupped her fullness and his clever fingertips teased the overly sensitive flesh.

Desire uncoiled deep inside her and spread a delicious warmth throughout her system. But warmth easily became a flame when he knelt before her and let his mouth take over for his hands. White hot sensation pierced straight through her soul while pure instinct had her back arching. Her legs threatened to collapse and she dug her fingers deep into his shoulders in an effort to find an anchor in the careening blackness tugging at her.

As he tasted at leisure, his hands were busy disposing of the rest of her clothing. As each article disappeared, his tender touch searched out new mysteries. She managed to stay on her feet by sheer will as he systematically exploited every nerve ending in her body. Heat suffused her from the inside out as she trembled with a need greater than anything she had ever imagined.

When he finally rose, apparently satisfied with his quest, he scooped her up into his arms. His clothing was rough against her bare skin, the contrast highly erotic. He walked a few steps and then stopped and leaned forward. She emitted a startled gasp as her arms tightened around his neck. The sensation of falling ended gently as she sank into a bed of cool linen. He left her and the inky blackness closed in around her, unsettling and vaguely threatening. Above the din of her own hammering pulse she thought she could hear the sound of his harsh breathing as he stripped away his clothing.

An unreasonable fear had her calling out his name. He came down beside her, and she immediately reached for him, needing to assure herself through touch that her veiled lover was indeed Cody. Her hands skimmed over the familiar planes of his chest and back. And then his mouth found hers and sent her spiraling out of control into the fierce vortex of passion. Time and space ceased to matter. Nothing existed for her beyond this misty, sensual world he'd created just for her. At this point in time he was the only world she needed.

He offered no tenderness now, and she asked for none. His hands were possessive and hard, and his mouth scorched her soft skin as he explored her willing body. He drove her ruthlessly, taking her on a wild roller coaster ride filled with mind shattering dips and heart stopping turns. Pleasure, nearly too intense to bear, overwhelmed her and carried her to heights previously unknown.

Near the pinnacle of fulfillment, he paused and demanded harshly, "Who's loving you, Katie?"

"Cody," she cried, her arms tightening around him. "Only Cody."

In the next heartbeat they were rushing together over the edge of madness and into a new dimension swirling with brilliant light and roaring sound.

Ten

Cody felt another delicate tremor race through her. Automatically, his arm tightened around her as one hand stroked rhythmically up and down her back. She sighed, her breath stirring the hair on his chest.

He was sure he had never been so completely sated in his life.

His first time with her had been fantastic. What they had just shared defied description. The lady had touched his soul, and he knew he'd never be the same again.

"Why is it so dark in here?" she asked drowsily.

"All the trees block out most of the light in this room. And there are dark curtains."

"It's a little unsettling," she admitted. "It was like having a phantom lover."

He chuckled softly. "A phantom lover," he repeated. "Would you like for me to turn the lights on?"

"Not just yet." She snuggled closer to him. "I'm still enjoying the illusion."

"As far as I'm concerned you could enjoy the illusion all night long. But I think I should remind you that I should be taking you home soon."

"I know. I've got two teenage daughters to think about. I know I have to set a proper example for them."

"You're a wonderful example," he assured her.

"Actually, I didn't have any trouble being a good example until I met you," she said thoughtfully. "You've corrupted me, Cody Washington."

"And enjoyed every minute of it."

She laughed softly. "Me, too."

He hugged her and dropped a kiss on her hair. This closeness was a new experience for him. He couldn't remember ever being tempted to linger like this. But then, Kathleen was different from the women he was used to being with. She was the kind of woman that a man could turn to during a cold winter night and find warmth. She was the kind of woman that had a man turning his back on his single lifestyle and looking forward to a shared future. And much to his amazement that was precisely where he found himself now.

He'd never been in love before, but he recognized the elusive sentiment for what it was. He was in deep, and sinking deeper with each moment he spent with her. His heart had been claimed by this woman who still had one foot in yesterday, even while she reached for tomorrow.

He closed his eyes and drew in a deep breath. He wanted her to know. He wanted to say the words, make it perfectly clear to her how he felt. But he knew it wouldn't be fair to her. She was just beginning to open up, beginning to find herself. He didn't doubt that she recognized what they had together as something special. He just doubted that she would want to make it a permanent arrangement.

"What's wrong?" she asked quietly, her hand caressing his arm. "I can feel the tension in you."

He shook his head and tried to shake off the mood. The first move had to come from her. She'd been bullied into situations her entire life. He wouldn't allow his love for her to do the same. He'd have to wait and see what time revealed.

"I need to take you home," he said. "It's probably close to two."

She rose up on her elbow and caressed his rough cheek with her hand. "Are you sure that's all it is? You're not upset with me?"

"Katie." Deep regret laced the single word. "I tend to have a short fuse most of the time. When I blew up tonight, it wasn't so much at you as it was your ex-husband. He's fed you a bunch of bull, and you've got to quit believing it."

"Give me time, Cody." Her fingertips traced his lips. "I'm making progress, but I still stumble. Help me see when I'm falling back on old habits, but don't get angry with me."

"I'm sorry," he whispered, his hands coming up to frame her face. "You're so special. I just want you to be as happy as you deserve to be."

She wound her arms around his neck and found his mouth with unerring ease. The embers from their earlier passion flared and spread like flames through a dry forest. Need, hot and persistent, overrode his logic, and he moaned with it.

"Just once more," she whispered frantically against his mouth. "Love me, Cody."

In one swift movement he rolled her to her back. "I do," he murmured hoarsely. "Always, Katie."

Days later, Kathleen could still hear those husky words echoing inside her mind. Was it possible that he'd let his true feelings show for that brief second? Or was she reading more into them than was there?

"Are you waiting for something to step out of the closet and ask you to wear it?" Holly asked curiously.

Kathleen snapped back to the present, aware of how foolish she must look as she stood gazing sightlessly into the closet. "That would be a help since I can't seem to make up my mind," she said ruefully.

Holly walked over and stood beside her. Without hesitating she reached in and came back out with a peach-colored silk blouse and matching slacks. "This looks nice on you," she stated.

"Thanks." Kathleen took the garments from her daughter.

Holly shrugged. "No problem." She walked over and stretched out on her stomach on the bed.

"Where's Heather?" Kathleen asked as she slipped into the blouse.

"Trying to put a call through to Daddy. I told her to come and get me if she got an answer."

Kathleen worked the pearl buttons through the buttonholes. Heather had been trying to reach Gary since the day Kathleen had broken her news about staying in Montana two weeks ago. Anger sizzled through Kathleen's veins. He was avoiding the situation. There was no way he'd go for two weeks and not check his messages even if he was out of town. Today would make Heather's fourth attempt to reach him. If he ignored her today of all days, Kathleen would be tempted to fly to Chicago and personally rip his cold heart out.

"Do you suppose he'll even remember it's our birthday?" Holly asked soberly.

Kathleen tucked her shirt into the waistband of her slacks and then closed the zipper. "I don't know," she said softly. "I can't figure him out anymore."

The door opened and Heather entered, a frown on her face. "Where can he be? What if something's happened to him? Who will know to call us?"

"Jackie knows," Holly reminded her.

"What if she was with Daddy and something happened?"

"Heather, there are plenty of people in Chicago who know where to contact us," Kathleen said calmly. "I'm sure your father is okay."

"Then why doesn't he call me back?" Heather dropped down on the edge of the bed. "I can't believe he hasn't gotten any of my messages. Why hasn't he called to wish us a happy birthday or sent us a present?"

Kathleen sighed as she ran a brush through her hair. "I honestly don't know, Heather."

"He's never forgotten before."

Because I was always there to remind him, Kathleen thought bitterly, and I didn't do it this time. Damn him. Why did he have to be so selfish when it came to the girls? Why couldn't he just once think of them first and himself second? Even as the questions filtered through her mind, she knew it was useless to try to answer them. There were no answers.

She turned from the mirror and pasted a bright smile on her face. "Let's just celebrate without him," she suggested. "You guys only turn fifteen once. We'll just party the night away and then tell him about it when he does call."

Holly rolled from the bed and stood up. "Sounds good to me," she said. She and her mother both looked at Heather.

The girl frowned for a moment longer and then a small smile curved her lips. "I did hear Mattie say that she and Lonny had baked a special cake for us."

"Oh really?" Kathleen's brow arched. "I'll bet it's fantastic."

"Everything Mattie fixes is fantastic," Holly stated.

"Well, let's go check it out," Heather said jumping to her feet, her sullen mood forgotten for the moment.

Mattie and Lonny carefully carried the huge sheet cake out of the kitchen. The crowd of people parted for them and they managed to reach the table without mishap. One half of the cake was chocolate with chocolate icing. The other half was white with white icing. The chocolate side was for Holly; the white for Heather. It boasted fifteen large flaming candles.

The girls took up positions on either side of the cake. Slowly, Heather counted to three and then they both blew with all their might. The flames were extinguished immediately as the crowd applauded.

The two girls pressed the palms of their right hands together. "Wish," they whispered in unison, closing their eyes. They stayed that way a moment, then opened their eyes and smiled at one another before drawing their hands apart.

Kathleen felt tears sting her eyes and blinked against the sudden urge to burst into tears. A hand touched her shoulder and she looked up into Cody's questioning eyes.

"What's that all about?" he asked.

She gave a shaky laugh. "Tradition. Gary taught them that on their first birthday. Amazingly, they remembered and have done it every year since. He called it a special twin wish."

Cody saw the tears in her eyes and gently ran his hand up and down her back. It was apparent to him in that instant that Gary Hunter still held a place in her life, whether he deserved to or not. Cody didn't like the feelings that thought generated. He was tempted to pull her close and brand her as his. But he knew she would never welcome the gesture in their present surroundings. And the need to do so unsettled him greatly. He had never been an insecure man. Yet he felt exactly that way with this woman.

"Mom, you get the first piece," Holly called. "Do you want white or chocolate?"

"Can I have both?"

"Sure."

Mattie served the cake and Lonny dipped the ice cream. Soon, all the guests and employees present were enjoying themselves. The twins made the rounds and chatted with everyone in the large dining hall. Kathleen knew how easily Holly had adapted to the ranch life and had heard from several of the guests and employees how easy she was to work with. But if this crowd was any indication, it appeared that Heather had scored a few points, too.

"Katie?"

Kathleen turned at the sharpness of Jon's voice calling to her. He was striding toward her, a scowl marring his features. She opened her mouth to respond at the same instant Heather let out a screech of excitement and darted across the room. A shocked numbness settled over Kathleen as she slowly rose to her feet and watched her daughter fly into the arms of the man following behind Jon.

Gary caught the girl close and declared, "You didn't think I'd forget your birthday, did you?"

"No, I knew you wouldn't. Why didn't you tell us you were coming?"

"I wanted to surprise you." He laughed as he set Heather back on her feet. Holly had moved slowly toward him, and he gave her a quizzical look. "You got a hug for your old man, Holly?"

She smiled slightly and offered an embrace that was degrees cooler than her sister's. When she drew away, his gaze shot back to Heather. "What the devil have you done to yourself?" he demanded.

Immediately, Heather's hand flew up to her hair. "Don't get mad," she said quickly. "I just wanted to try something different. It'll grow out."

His look was skeptical. "It's not going to stay that color, is it?"

She laughed. "No. It's only temporary."

"Good." He gave a quick laugh. "At least I can tell you two apart now," he teased.

"Oh, Daddy!" Heather reached up and kissed his cheek again. "I'm so glad you came. You've made the day perfect."

He lifted his head and Kathleen felt his dark eyes slice right through her. In a few seconds his gaze scanned the small group behind her. From Jon standing almost protectively at her side, to Olan and Jenny observing curiously, to Cody still sitting casually in the chair beside hers. Those sharp eyes seemed to take a careful measure of Cody before flashing back to her.

Gary crossed the room, a lazy smile curving his generous mouth. "Hello, Kathleen," he greeted smoothly. In a totally unexpected move he bent and brushed a kiss across her lips. She instantly jerked away. His smile widened and he said silkily, "Surprised?"

"Why didn't you let me know you were coming?" she asked, her voice strained.

"And spoil my surprise?" He cocked one brow. "It was more fun this way, don't you think?"

No, I don't, Kathleen wanted to scream at him. It wasn't fair that he would appear without warning. Dealing with him on the phone was one thing. Dealing with him in person was quite another. She wasn't ready for this. Already she felt at a distinct disadvantage. Already she felt the old buttons being pushed.

As usual, he looked like he could have just stepped off the cover of a fashion magazine. His thick dark hair was cut short and styled to perfection. He'd been blessed with movie star handsome features. A custom made black silk shirt emphasized his broad shoulders and pleated gray slacks accentuated lean hips. There was no denying that he was a handsome man. But Kathleen knew that it was just a mask that hid an ugliness that few had witnessed.

Heather took his hand. "How long can you stay?" she asked anxiously.

"Oh, I've got several days free," he replied vaguely. "I thought I'd see what it was your mother found so exciting out here." His gaze made one suspicious sweep of Cody before looking back to Kathleen. "You don't mind, do you, Kathleen?"

Heather quickly filled the silence her mother let stretch out. "Of course she doesn't mind. Where are you staying?"

Gary cast his ex-wife a mocking glance before turning to his daughter. "Surely, I can find a room around here for a few days?"

Heather turned immediately to Jon. "He can stay at the house, can't he, Uncle Jon? You've got another free room, don't you?"

Jon shot his sister a desperate look. It was Holly who stepped in and suggested easily, "Maybe you'd be more comfortable with a motel room in Bozeman, Dad. You'd have better access to a phone and a little more privacy. Things are a little crowded at the house, with only one bathroom and all."

"Oh, I don't know." Gary seemed to consider. "I think I might enjoy roughing it out here for a few days."

Cody saw Kathleen sway slightly and came instantly to his feet. He had the distinct impression that Gary Hunter was playing some kind of mind game with his ex-wife. If she wasn't going to end it, he damn well would.

He stepped up behind Kathleen and placed a hand at the small of her back. He nearly swore as he felt her tremble. "We haven't met," he said tersely to the man regarding him smugly. "I'm Cody Washington."

"Gary Hunter." His forehead creased. "I don't think Kathleen's told me about you. Are you one of the cowboys on the ranch?"

"You could say that," Cody returned blandly. "If you'll excuse us, Kathleen was just going to retrieve something from the house for me."

As if emerging from a dream she looked up into his face, frowning. "What?"

Cody's hand urged her forward. "You were going to get that book for me." She started to protest, but his fingers closed insistently around her elbow. Obediently, she followed his prompting. As they crossed the room, she was vaguely aware of Heather making introductions.

Once outside, Kathleen drew in a deep gulp of air. "Where are we going?" she asked, feeling as if a fog was clearing from her brain.

"Anywhere to get you the hell away from him," Cody growled.

Their final destination ended up being Jon's den. Cody ushered her inside and closed the door none too gently. When he turned to her, his eyes were green chips of ice.

"Are you going to let him treat you like that?" he demanded. "He's on your home turf now, Kathleen. You don't have to bend to his will anymore."

"I. . . . I know," she stammered. Nervously, she raked a hand through her hair. "He caught me off guard, that's all."

"That's all? Hell, he nearly annihilated you without breaking a sweat. What is it about him that makes you cower like that?"

"I suppose it's habit!" she cried. "Why are you shouting at me?"

"Because you need someone to. Why can't you stand up to him? God knows you have no trouble challenging me every step of the way."

"You're not him."

"And I never will be," he said flatly. An uneasy silence settled between them. Kathleen, unable to meet the accusation in his eyes any longer, turned away and walked to the window. She stood there, her hands moving up and down her arms as if trying to chase away a chill.

Cody drew in a calming breath and walked over to Jon's desk. He leaned there a moment, contemplating her. How the hell could he get it across to her that it nearly killed him to see all the spark go out of her in the presence of her ex-husband? He much preferred the anger between them now than the submissiveness he'd watched develop before his eyes in the dining hall.

Cody rubbed his hands over his face and sighed deeply. "No one can do it for you, Kathleen," he said wearily. "You have to help yourself."

"I know."

"He's going to use Heather to his advantage."

"I know that, too."

"Well, if you know all that," he said sharply, "then you might want to start thinking about where he's going to be staying. If you don't speak up, you're going to end up with your ex-husband as a house guest. Can you handle that?"

"It'll be okay," she said, pensively. "It'll give the girls more time with him and. . . ."

The sound of his fist slamming heavily against Jon's desk had her whirling around. He crossed to her in three long strides and caught her by her upper arms. Her heart jumped into her throat as she stared up into a fury she'd never seen in him before.

"Stop it!" he thundered. "Damn it, Kathleen. Why do you continue to make excuses for him? How far will you continue to bend before he finally breaks you? Don't you have an ounce of pride left?"

Like a flame set to a tinderbox, fierce emotion exploded inside her. She shoved him hard, causing him to stumble back and instantly release her. "You don't know anything about it!" she cried. "He stripped me of my pride years ago, and I'll bend as far as I need to to survive his visit." She raked a trembling hand through her hair. "You think you've got all of the answers, Cody, but you don't. You see everything as simple black and white, but my relationship with Gary is not that simple. It's just not that easy."

"It'll never get easier if you won't stand up to him. You've got to. . . ."

"Oh, stop it!" she shouted, bringing her hands up to cover her ears. "Quit pushing me! I can't be the woman you want me to be. And I can't handle any more pressure from you. I need your support. Why can't you just give it to me?"

"I can't support you when you won't even fight him." He turned and strode toward the door. "If you want to handle it by letting him continue to walk all over you, go right ahead." He paused with his hand on the doorknob and sent her one last blazing look. "Just don't expect me to stick around and watch. I don't have the stomach for it."

As the door slammed behind him, an uncontrollable sob ripped through her. Why couldn't he understand how she felt? Because you've never told him, a tiny voice reminded her. Cody knew nothing about her true relationship with Gary because she'd consciously chosen not to tell him. Just as she'd chosen not to tell anyone else over the years.

Confession was a risk she'd never been able to take. She was convinced that no one, Cody included, would ever be able to understand why she had made the choices she had. It was all too painful, too shameful to talk about.

Now, with Cody gone, it wouldn't matter anyway.

Eleven

Kathleen was surprised when she'd arrived at the museum on Saturday morning and found Cody already there. After their argument of the previous evening she hadn't really expected to see him. She should have known better. He may have been angry with her, but he wasn't the kind of man to let his personal feelings interfere with a commitment he'd already made. After all, the museum was important to him.

She couldn't help the little spark of hope that flared as she stepped into the entryway. Maybe they'd have a chance to talk, a chance to go back over some of the things they'd said last night. She'd thought about it all well into the night. In the final analysis she'd come to the conclusion that she wished she'd had the courage to tell Cody about her life with Gary. Telling him would bring back all the pain and shame she'd wanted desperately to forget. But telling him might make it easier for him to understand why she didn't have the strength that he thought she should have.

She moved through the quiet rooms until she found him. He was staining the new woodwork that would go around the doors and windows. He was so intent on his work that he obviously hadn't heard her come in. She stood in the doorway and studied his profile highlighted by the strong morning light pouring in through the long window. She thought he looked a little tired and wondered if he'd spent a sleepless night, too. It seemed like a cruel thing to wish for, but she hoped that their argument had disturbed him as much as it had her. She hoped he cared that much.

His head snapped up suddenly, his green eyes instantly locking on her. Irritation flashed there sharply, before he lowered his head and went back to work. "You startled me," he said.

Kathleen felt her small reserve of hope start to dwindle. His greeting wasn't exactly promising. "Sorry," she said quietly. He didn't acknowledge her apology, just continued to apply the stain to the wood with smooth even strokes.

She took a couple of steps into the room. "It looks like you're about done with all that. Have you been here long?"

"A couple of hours. I'm about done staining. Tomorrow I'll cut the wood and nail it up."

"It looks nice."

"Oak wood always does."

He hadn't even looked at her. Was it that easy for him to push her out of his life? After all they'd shared, could he just ignore her, or worse yet, reduce their relationship to that of polite acquaintances? Was she destined to spend her life in Montana close to the man who meant so much to her, knowing he would never accept her because she wasn't strong enough for him.

"Cody. . . ." He looked at her and her voice faltered as a truth surer than anything she'd ever known slammed into her. She loved him. She stared at him as the words raced around inside her head. She'd known so little real love in her life, how could she be sure of what she was feeling? Panic set her pulse flying as she tried to think clearly. She loved him? Could it be the real, forever after, total commitment love she'd only read about? Oh, yes, a tiny voice assured her firmly.

Cody straightened, a frown creasing his features. "Kathleen, are you okay?"

She wanted to laugh. She wanted to cry. "Cody, I. . . ." She stopped, feeling as if a brick wall had just sprung up before her. What was she doing? Did she really think he would appreciate her blurting out that she loved him? Did she really think that she would be the first to utter those classic words to him? The man was thirty-eight years old and single by choice. Was she really naive enough to think that he'd never been in love before, that she'd be the first for him? And did she really think a man like Cody Washington would want a woman laden with as much emotional baggage as she was?

"Kathleen. . . ."

"Cody, are you here?"

Kathleen was snapped out of her fog by the unfamiliar voice echoing through the empty rooms. Cody stepped around his work and shot her a quick look. "That's Randy Myers here to do the floors. Let me get him started, then we can finish this conversation."

"No. It's nothing important. Just forget it." She turned away before she made a complete fool of herself. A moment later she heard him leave the room. Drawing in a painful breath, she left the room in the opposite direction and headed upstairs.

Kathleen paused in her painting and listened as Cody talked with the electrician about checking out the wiring and installing new track lighting. For a moment she let the deep timbre of Cody's voice wash over her as it drifted up the stairs. She thought his voice sounded deeper than usual and wondered if he was catching something.

She sighed as she went back to painting the room that would eventually be her office. If he was coming down with something, he hadn't seen a need to confide in her. After three days, she was enduring his cool responses and guarded attitude toward her. She was enduring, but she hadn't found a way to stop the pain that pierced her heart.

She bent and balanced her paintbrush on the edge of the paint tray. Turning, she walked to the window and stood gazing out over the lush, wild scenery. Three days had passed since she'd made the heart stopping discovery about her feelings for him, and still she didn't know what to do. She loved him, but she couldn't be the woman he wanted her to be. She'd never been strong. Gary had known that about her from the very beginning and had used it to his advantage for fifteen years. She couldn't change who she was. She simply couldn't stand up to Gary like Cody thought she should. Sadly, it appeared that that weakness was the one thing Cody couldn't forgive.

She leaned her forehead against the cool glass and wished she had someone to talk to about all the confusing thoughts roaming around inside her head. While Cody was establishing a growing distance between them, her ex-husband seemed to be vying for the Father of the Year Award. Since his arrival he'd been so attentive to the girls that even Holly had relaxed her guard somewhat. Heather was eagerly basking in the extra attention.

Kathleen was suspicious. Gary had always been a kind of chameleon, able to change his colors to suit his current situation. She couldn't help but wonder what he was up to.

For the most part she'd steered clear of him. In addition to the time he was spending with the girls on the ranch, he'd also taken them into Bozeman for a movie and some shopping. Tomorrow he planned to take them to Yellowstone for the day. Kathleen had been invited to join them on that trip, but she'd declined. Heather's disappointment had been obvious, but Kathleen wasn't about to fall into that trap. The last thing she needed was for Heather to start weaving fantasies about her parents getting back together. No matter how wonderful Gary was coming across during this visit, Kathleen would never entertain the idea of going back to him.

Freedom had been hard earned and had become too sweet. She would think long and hard about giving it up again. Unless Cody asked, a little voice whispered in the back of her mind. The thought startled her and she straightened. Would she give up her freedom for him? The answer was an unwavering yes. In many ways she'd found her freedom with him. She'd learned more about herself since meeting him than she had in the entire thirty-four years of her life. If she could just make him understand. . . .

"Kathleen?"

She jerked around, the subject of her thoughts standing just inside the doorway. She felt her cheeks heat as if he could read her mind.

"I'm done for the day," he said. "The electrician is still here. Are you going to stay for a while?"

"Sure. I want to finish this room."

He nodded "I won't be over tomorrow. Jon and I have some things to see to on the ranch."

"Okay." She hesitated and frowned as he started to turn away. "Cody, are you okay?" She shrugged as his green eyes seemed to bore into her. "You've been coughing. You sound like you might be catching something."

"I'm okay," he said evenly. For a moment his gaze held hers; then he abruptly turned away. "I'll try to get back over here on Wednesday," he called over his shoulder.

She listened to his retreating footsteps and fought back the tears that burned in her chest. How could she have been so foolish? Hadn't she learned anything over the years? Love didn't exist for her; it never had, it never would. She'd left herself wide open for this pain when she'd allowed herself to believe that what she and Cody had was different. But there was no difference here. Once again she'd fallen short of the expectations laid out for her. Once again she'd been less than perfect.

Cody couldn't sleep—again. He rolled out of bed and pulled on jeans and a work shirt. The sun wouldn't be up for another hour, but it wouldn't do him any good to stay in bed. Sleep had been an elusive mistress the last few days, teasing him with a couple of hours of blissful oblivion before dancing away to leave him wide awake with his doubts and self-recriminations.

It was no more than he deserved, he decided as he headed to the kitchen and went about preparing a pot of coffee. He'd hurt Kathleen. He could see it every time he looked into her eyes. But he couldn't bring himself to make things right with her. Just the thought of her staying in the same house with her ex-husband sent disgust swirling through Cody's stomach. Why would she allow the man to bulldoze her like that? What kind of hold did he still have over her?

Cody leaned back against the counter and reached up to rub his forehead. He had a colossal headache this morning and hadn't had that first drink to justify it. It seemed to go along with the rest of the aches his body was sporting, both physical and mental. Mentally, he was exhausted. Physically, he was getting there. He couldn't continue to put in fourteen and sixteen hour days with only two or three hours worth of sleep.

He moved across the room to the window facing the back of the main house. Gradually, the darkness receded reminding him of the sunrise he'd shared with Kathleen. Despite his fatigue, his body responded easily to the memory of their loving that morning. He would have given anything right then just to be able to hold her. She belonged to him. At least the part of her that wasn't still Gary's belonged to him.

Cody swore softly and turned away from the window. He'd just faced his biggest fear. What if Kathleen wasn't over Gary? What if she still felt something for the man? Logically, Cody couldn't imagine how she could feel anything but loathing for a man who had treated her as Gary had. But Cody also knew that emotions were seldom logical.

Which was why he'd decided to put some distance between himself and Kathleen. He knew without a doubt that he loved her. He also knew he couldn't compete with whatever hold her ex-husband had over her. Kathleen had to be free of her past before she could look to any kind of future. And for some reason that Cody didn't even come close to understanding, she was still very much bound by the past and her ex-husband. After witnessing her reaction to Gary's surprise arrival the other evening, Cody had seriously begun to wonder if she would ever be truly free.

He poured a cup of coffee and relished the first sip, hoping it would ease some of the tightness in his chest. He really did feel like hell. The cold he'd been fighting was obviously winning. If he could just get some rest. . . . Well, it didn't matter anyway. He'd promised Jon his help today.

Maybe by the time his head hit the pillow tonight, sleep would be a little more accommodating.

"You've done a fine job of avoiding me, Kathleen."

Kathleen felt a chill skitter down her spine as Gary stepped out of Jon's office and directly into her path. She stared at him silently, a basket of clean laundry between them. Thinking she had the house to herself, she'd been on her way upstairs to put it away in her room.

"I haven't been avoiding you," she said coolly. "I've been busy. Just like I am now." She arched a brow. "Excuse me."

The grandfather clock at the end of the hallway ticked off the seconds as Gary studied her, and every nerve in her body screamed for him to let her pass. With a benign smile he stepped aside, allowing her to continue up the stairs. About half way up she realized he was right behind her. Her heart gave a startled lurch, but she fought down the panic that threatened her.

"I think I have to insist that we talk," he said as they reached the landing.

She turned to him before opening her door. "Fine. Wait for me downstairs, and I'll be right there."

"Nah." He reached around her and pushed her bedroom door open. "We're already here."

She glared at him as her pulse picked up an uneven tempo. He laughed softly at her obvious discomfort. "Come on, Kathleen," he cajoled. "What are you so afraid of?"

"I'm not afraid."

"No?" His fingers lifted and traced the skin along her neck until he found the tell-tale beat there. "Is it desire then that has your pulse hammering this way?"

She jerked away and walked into the room. His innuendo and touch had her stomach churning. Fear had the blood chilling in her veins. She dropped the laundry onto the seat of the wicker rocker and turned back to him. The door closed with a soft click when he leaned back against it.

"All this fresh mountain air must agree with you, Kathleen," he said thoughtfully. "You've become quite lovely." He tilted his head to the side and studied her a bit longer. "Maybe it isn't the air after all. Maybe it has more to do with that cowboy you were with when I arrived the other night. Tell me, Kathleen, have you taken a lover?"

"My personal life is no longer any of your business." Her voice was even, concealing her fear.

He shrugged. "Technically, you're right. But I'm really very curious." He pushed away from the door and crossed to her. His hand came up to cup her chin, and he stared down into her eyes. "Have you finally learned how to respond to a man? Or did he find you as disappointing as I always have?"

She flinched, feeling the sting of his words as distinctly as a slap. She hated herself instantly for the reaction. He had no power over her. He couldn't hurt her unless she let him.

He chuckled, a low hateful sound she'd heard too many times over the years and still heard in her nightmares. "Did you really think it would be any different with another man?" he chided unkindly. "You know you don't have what it takes to please a man. You never have. You never will."

Tears sprang to her eyes as his words sank into her brain like the insidious poison it was. But a new voice echoed inside her head, rejecting the words. "Don't listen to him. He's lying to you. You know he's lying." Cody's voice. Cody's support.

"Let go of me."

Gary arched a brow at her weak show of assertiveness. "When I'm ready," he murmured. "I think I want to see if your stud was able to teach you anything."

He bent toward her, and she stood very still. When his mouth covered hers, she remained motionless. He finally lifted his head and sighed. "Ah, Kathleen," he admonished. "I don't think you're even trying. Let's try it again with a little more feeling. Okay?"

He moved toward her again, and she twisted her face away. His fingers tightened painfully on her jaw, forcing her back. "You can't win, Kathleen," he warned darkly. "I'm much stronger, you know."

Oh, she knew all right. He'd only used force with her on a few occasions, and that was because she was a quick study. She'd learned early on that it was much wiser to submit without a fight. His forte was verbal coercion. He liked to scare her. Just as he was doing now.

"He can only hurt you if you let him," the voice inside her head reminded her. "Don't let him hurt you. Don't let him scare you."

She stared into his eyes boldly, forcing back the panic that had her heart racing. "Your days of bullying me are over, Gary."

"I don't see anyone here to stop me now," he challenged.

"I'm warning you. Let go of me."

His eyes widened before he threw back his head and laughed. "God, that's impressive, Kathleen. You're warning me? Should I be scared?"

"If you're smart," she said flatly.

Instantly, all humor faded and his brow lowered. He searched her eyes as if looking for a real threat behind her words. She met his gaze straight on and fought against the quaking that threatened to take over her body. Instinctively she knew that if she was going to survive this encounter, she couldn't show fear.

After what seemed to be an eternity, he released her abruptly and pushed her away. She balanced herself against the arm of the rocker as he swung away and slashed a hand through his hair.

"Hell, why should I even bother?" he growled. "I've had you enough to know it's not worth the trouble."

Relief rolled through her like the ocean at high tide. She'd done it. She'd broken the abusive cycle that she'd become trapped in years ago. For the first time, she'd met him on his own level and had beaten him. She'd won and wanted to shout with her victory.

He turned around to face her and slipped his hands into his pants pockets. "You need to do something about Heather," he said casually, as if the last few minutes had not passed between them.

She straightened, forcing her weak knees to support her and

prayed that her voice wouldn't betray her inner turmoil. "I think you need to be the one to deal with Heather."

"No, you're the one hell-bent on uprooting her and moving her out here. You tell her that she can't come live with me."

Kathleen shrugged. "Why can't she? She's your daughter, too."

Gary laughed sharply and shook his head. "But I never wanted either one of them," he admitted bluntly. "The child I wanted you killed."

The attack was so completely unexpected and ruthless it sent her mind reeling. She stared at him as her mental process began to automatically close down. In an instant she understood. She hadn't won after all. He was still holding the trump card—the one thing that she could never stand against.

"What really happened that day, Kathleen?" he asked, his voice low and full of raw malice. "Did Kevin cry out that morning and you just didn't go to check on him? Or did you help him along a little to that tiny grave?"

She closed her eyes and shook her head. "No," she whispered as the horror came rushing back at her in vivid detail. "It was crib death. The coroner confirmed it."

"That's what you convinced everyone of, isn't it. Except me. I know the truth. I know that you killed my son. You wanted to get back at me and that was the only way you could do it. I know, Kathleen. I know. You murdered your own baby."

Emotions buried in the deepest regions of her soul bubbled upward, erupting with the force of a volcanic explosion. Caught up in the avalanche of pain, she was unaware that it was her voice screaming the word "no" over and over again. Blindly she flew at the source of her torment, her fists flailing against his chest wildly.

She didn't realize that it was Cody who flew through the door and forcefully pulled her away, wrapped his arms tightly around her and held her close to his body. Just as she didn't realize that it was his soothing words that tried to calm her.

She was unaware of everything but the searing pain that seemed to have ripped a hole in her soul. Over time she had managed to bury the memories of Kevin along with the devastating heartache she'd suffered. To pretend it all had never happened was the only way she'd been able to survive. Pretending worked until Gary brought the painful memories back to life with his ugly, hateful words, leaving her to deal all over again with a burden that had never been reconciled in her mind.

Cody's arms tightened around Kathleen as another shiver worked its way through her body. He was leaned back against the headboard of her bed with her curled against him as if he could protect her from all the demons that pursued her.

The truth of the matter was he had never felt so useless. He couldn't protect her from an enemy he couldn't see. He would have liked to get his hands on Gary Hunter's neck. But Jon had wisely hustled the man from the room and most likely from the house. After what Jon and Cody had witnessed, Gary would be wise to stay as far away from the Four Aces Ranch as possible.

Cody closed his eyes and rested his head back against the wall. Pain was throbbing in his forehead and he felt awful, but he wasn't about to leave Kathleen until he was sure she was okay.

"You must think I'm a real coward."

He tilted his head forward to look down at her. She hadn't moved when she'd spoken and her words had been so quiet he'd barely heard them. His hand came up to stroke her hair.

"No, I don't," he murmured.

"I tried to stand up to him," she whispered against his chest. "I even thought I was winning." She gave a trembling laugh. "God, what a fool I am. I can't win against him. I can't."

"Katie." Cody drew her closer, unsure of what to say to her. He hurt for her, but he didn't know how to help her.

"I didn't kill my baby." Her voice shook with the force of her emotions. "I could never have done that."

"I know. Tell me about it," he urged gently.

She drew in a fortifying breath. "His name was Kevin, and he would be five this October. He was such a beautiful baby, so happy and content. Giving birth to him was the only thing I ever did that pleased Gary." She paused and her fingers worked nervously at one of the buttons on Cody's shirt. She worked it back and forth, up and down. "Gary lavished more attention on that baby in the two short months of his life than he had on the girls in their full ten years." Her voice broke and Cody pressed his cheek against her forehead.

"It's okay," he whispered.

She fought for control before continuing. "One morning I put Kevin down for his nap and he didn't wake up. He just went to sleep forever. He was gone, and I couldn't get him to come back." Cody felt her tears wet his shirt and chill his skin. He would have given anything to take her pain from her, would have done anything to spare her the memory.

"Gary blamed me," she said harshly. "He never thought I took good enough care of the baby. Somehow he came up with the notion that I'd actually killed Kevin. Even though the coroner listed the cause of death as Sudden Infant Death Syndrome, Gary still continues to accuse me of harming my own child. The months following Kevin's death were the worst. Gary kept up a constant campaign of accusations until I thought I'd lose my mind. His mind games became so devious that I didn't want to live anymore. If I hadn't had the girls. . . ." Her voice broke off at the same instant the button she'd been twisting came off in her fingers. The sentence went unfinished, but Cody felt the chilling certainty of her words touch his soul.

"It's okay," he assured her, stroking his hand down her hair. He had to force himself to stay calm and continue to hold her. Every instinct he had was urging him to find Gary Hunter and square Kathleen's account for her.

"Gary's always enjoyed playing mind games with me," she continued hollowly. Cody closed his eyes, not wanting to hear any more, but unable to leave her. "At first I was so young and naive I didn't even realize what he was doing. By the time I did know, I didn't really care anymore. I was in a trap that I saw no way out of. He never made it any secret that he was disappointed with the girls, and I was afraid for them at first. But he has never treated them cruelly, other than being stingy with his time and attention." Her fingers had moved to another button, and he felt emotion shiver through her. "I guess I was the only entertainment he needed."

Cody swallowed hard and felt his stomach knot as deep regret washed over him. How idealistic he must have sounded as he'd blithely passed judgment on her life and her way of dealing with it. Idealistic and naive. He'd been so sure that she could easily overcome Gary's influence if she truly wanted to. God, his arrogance was disgusting and embarrassing. He'd pushed her to make immediate changes, when in all actuality those changes would take years. How could she ever forgive him? How could he ever make it up to her?

"I tried to be strong, Cody," she murmured, her voice husky now. "I wanted to be strong for you. I wanted to show you that I could stand up to him. I just couldn't quite pull it off. I'm sorry I can't be what you want me to be."

"No, Katie." He tilted her head back and looked down into tear drenched blue eyes. He felt his heart break, physically felt it shatter in his chest. "You're perfect," he said, his voice rough with raw emotion. "I was wrong, Katie. I didn't understand what you were up against. I'm sorry. Please forgive me."

"I should have told you about it, but I wanted so badly just to forget." A sad smile curved her lips and she reached up to caress his cheek. "You made me feel so special I just didn't want any of the ugliness from the past to touch what we had."

"Katie." He closed his eyes and bent to press a kiss to her forehead. Words eluded him. What could he possibly say to her now?

"Thank you for staying with me," she said with a sigh. She dropped her hand and settled her cheek back against his chest. "The worst thing about Kevin's death was that there was no one there to hold me," she said. "I was so alone. There was no one there to hold me like this."

Cody had nothing to say to that. It was just as well considering the fact that he couldn't speak at that particular moment. Hot emotion burned in his throat and behind his eyes. He wanted to make everything right for her and knew he never could. He couldn't change the past and couldn't guarantee her future. At this point all he could do was hold her.

Gradually he felt her body relax and grow heavy against his. Her breathing deepened and still he continued to hold her. He didn't want to leave her. He wanted her to sleep peacefully in his arms, as if his presence could chase away any of the demons that might follow her into sleep.

Sometime later, a hand settled on his shoulder, and he looked up into Mattie's dark eyes. He must have dozed because the room was drenched with late evening shadows.

"She's asleep," Mattie whispered. "Come downstairs, Cody."

He nodded and moved stiffly, trying to ease away from Kathleen without disturbing her sleep. Carefully, he settled her back against the pillow. She didn't even murmur when he tucked the covers around her shoulders. For a long moment, he stood and gazed down at her before turning to follow Mattie out.

"Are you okay?" Mattie asked as they moved down the staircase. At the bottom she turned to him and laid a hand against his forehead. "You're running a fever," she announced.

"I'm okay." He moved around her and stepped into the den. Jon was there. Cody dropped into a chair and reached up to rub his pounding head.

"What happened to Hunter?" he asked.

"I strongly suggested that he find some place to stay in Bozeman. He didn't argue."

"Did you break any bones?"

"I wanted to but Mattie wouldn't let me."

"That's a damn shame," Cody muttered.

"It wouldn't have solved anything," Mattie said logically. "Getting him out of this house was the best thing to do."

"Getting him out of this state would be even better." Cody lifted his head and was surprised to feel the world swing a little out of focus.

"You're sick," Mattie said instantly. "You need to be in bed. Let Jon drive you home."

Cody shook his head. "Lightning is in the barn. I'll be okay."

"You're a stubborn man," Mattie stated. "Will you at least eat before you go?"

He shook his head and pushed to his feet. "I'll get something at home." He ignored the glare she sent his way and looked at Jon. "Did you know Kathleen was involved in an abusive relationship?"

The blunt question caught Jon off guard. His eyes widened. "Physically?"

"I'm not sure, but he dished out enough mental abuse over the years to warp anyone. Did you know about the baby boy that died?"

Jon shook his head and dropped heavily into his chair. "Dear God," he breathed. "When? How?"

"Five years ago. Sudden Infant Death Syndrome." Cody leaned against a chair. "Gary has accused her of killing the baby. I guess he does it every chance he gets. It's just one of the mind games he likes to play with her."

"I didn't know," Jon whispered. "I should have known, but I didn't."

Cody drew in a deep breath and let it out slowly. "Now you know," he said wearily. "Your little sister has been living in hell for the last fifteen years. Keep that bastard away from her. And I'd keep an eye on the girls, too. At this point, I wouldn't trust him not to hurt them no matter what Kathleen says."

Jon nodded. "I'll take care of things."

Cody turned and headed for the door. Things were getting fuzzy around the edges. Hopefully, the fresh air would help clear away some of the cobwebs on the way home.

"Cody, please be careful," Mattie called.

He lifted his hand in response before disappearing out the door.

Twelve

Somewhere in the deep recesses of his mind, Cody identified the barrage of noise as an insistent pounding on his front door. Initially, he'd thought it was just an extension of the throbbing in his head. Now he realized the noise was only aggravating his throbbing head.

Swearing soundly, he climbed out of bed and pulled on the jeans he had discarded yesterday. He zipped them but didn't bother with the snap as he stumbled barefoot down the hallway.

"I'm coming," he barked when the pounding became too much for him to bear. He jerked the door open ready to spill blood, but found himself caught in a fit of coughing instead.

"You look like hell," Jon observed bluntly.

"Go away." Cody moved to push the door closed, but Jon's hand blocked the maneuver.

"I guess Mattie was right." Jon's glance took in everything from the disheveled hair and day old beard to the hastily donned jeans and bare feet. He stepped inside and closed the door.

Cody had turned away and was headed for the kitchen. "You better watch out," he warned. "I'm probably contagious."

"No doubt." Jon leaned a shoulder against the doorjamb leading into the kitchen and kept a safe distance. "I brought Lightning home."

"Thanks." Cody reached inside the refrigerator and pulled out a bottle of orange juice. He unscrewed the lid and drank directly from the container. Taking it with him, he walked over and dropped into one of the chairs at the table. "When I went to leave your place yesterday I found I couldn't keep my balance in the saddle. Damned annoying," he muttered lifting the bottle to his mouth again.

"Earl said he brought you home. It's nearly seven. You been in bed all day?"

Cody threw a quick glance out the window noticing the long evening shadows. "Guess so." He pressed his fingers to his eyes.

"My guess is you're not feeling a whole lot better."

Cody gave a humorless laugh. "It's just the flu. Nothing fatal." He coughed again and Jon arched a dubious brow.

"Have you considered seeing a doctor?"

"I'll be okay." If he was ever able get rid of the to throbbing in his head and the fever that seemed to constantly fluctuate, he might survive. At this point, he wasn't so sure passing on to the other side would be such a bad thing.

"Is Kathleen okay?" he asked, wishing he could have seen her today. There were things he needed to say; things she needed to hear.

"She's fine. We haven't heard anything from Gary today. We're hoping he went back to Chicago."

Cody nodded and took another long drink of juice.

"Is Jenny checking on you?" Jon asked, truly concerned by his friend's flushed face and obvious discomfort.

"She and Dad are in Los Angeles until. . . ." His voice trailed off as he struggled to come up with a day. Hell, he couldn't even remember what day it was.

"When are they due back, Cody?" Jon prompted.

"Thursday, I think."

"That's tomorrow. I'll send Mattie over with something to eat in a little while."

"Don't bother. I can't eat." Cody rested his head against his folded arms. His fever was back. He could feel the waves of heat radiating from his body.

"What if I send Kathleen?"

His head jerked up and he grimaced as the pain momentarily intensified. "Don't send anyone," he said through clenched teeth.

"You know as soon as Mattie finds out you're sick, she'll be over here."

"Don't tell her." Cody pushed his chair back and stood unsteadily. "Have mercy on me, Jon, and just leave me alone. I'm bound to be better tomorrow."

Jon stood back and watched as Cody made his way carefully down the hallway. "I'll check on you tomorrow."

There was no answer.

Cody was determined to feel better. After more than thirty-six hours in bed he declared himself healed. A hot shower eased some of the aches in his body and a light breakfast helped appease the hollow feel of his stomach. The fever seemed to be gone and the throbbing in his head had faded to a vague pounding. His chest still hurt when he coughed, but he figured as long as he was on his feet, he was definitely improving.

He stepped out onto the front porch and let his gaze adjust to the hazy sunlight. The morning was half gone and the clouds gathering on the western horizon indicated a change in the weather. It was still a pretty morning even if it was a little more brisk than usual for this time of the year.

He finished off the rest of his orange juice and carried the glass back into the house. Moments later he emerged again, his hat in hand. He didn't feel up to a lot of strenuous activity, but a day spent in the sunlight was an appealing idea. He'd take Lightning and head up to the north ridge to check on the fences there. It was an easy ride and he could be back well before Olan and Jenny were due home later that afternoon. As always, he left a message on their answering machine indicating what his plans were.

He needed the fresh mountain air to blow some of the cobwebs out of his brain. Kathleen had haunted his fevered sleep, and he knew he had to take the time to order his thoughts. Despite his illness one thing had become very clear to him over the last week. He wanted Kathleen in his life—permanently. He loved her, and he was going to make sure she knew it before another week was up.

With his resolve firmly in place, he settled his hat on his head and headed for the stables.

* * *

Dark clouds were moving in from the west when Kathleen returned from the museum late in the afternoon. As she hurried toward the front porch of the ranch house she felt the chill in the air. The wind had picked up and thunder rumbled faintly in the distance.

She stepped into the entry hall and was immediately aware of the voices drifting out from Jon's office. When the front door closed behind her with a definite thud the voices all went silent.

"Katie?" Jon called.

She stepped into the doorway seeing that Earl and Joe were also present in the room. Her greeting took them all in before she looked at her brother expectantly.

"Come in for a minute," he said, his gaze seeming to study her intently. Kathleen noted his solemn perusal and felt a faint prickle of alarm shoot along her spine.

She moved into the room and sent him a hesitant smile. "What's up?"

"Why don't you sit down a minute," he suggested quietly.

Something was definitely wrong. She shot a glance to Earl and Joe and neither of them met her eyes. "What's happened?" she demanded. "Just tell me."

"We can't find Heather," Jon said flatly. "No one has seen her since about eleven."

Kathleen checked her watch. "That's just five hours. Maybe she went on one of the all day trail rides."

Jon shook his head. "They all left earlier than that. Besides they're all back because of the bad weather rolling in. No one has seen her."

Kathleen felt things get a little fuzzy around the edges. Her first thought was that Gary had come and taken her with him. After everything that had happened, she wouldn't have been surprised if he tried to pull something like that.

"We're pretty sure she's taken a horse and gone off somewhere."

"But where would she go?" Kathleen asked vaguely. "I mean, where is there to go?"

"I don't know. I've sent someone over to check the Washington place. She might have gone there. But Olan and Jenny aren't due

back from Los Angeles until later this afternoon and Cody has
been sick. I don't. . . ."

"Cody's sick?" she asked suddenly. "What's wrong?"

"Flu, I guess. I saw him yesterday and he'd been in bed all day.
From the looks of him then, I doubt that he's a whole lot better
today."

That explained why he hadn't been back to help her at the museum for the last two days. She couldn't help the twinge of relief
she felt. She had begun to wonder if she'd imagined his words
when he'd held her following her encounter with Gary. She thought
he might have changed his mind after all. But if he'd been ill, that
would explain his absence.

She turned her attention back to Jon. "Do you really think she
would have gone there?"

He sighed and shook his head. "She took provisions: water, blankets and some clothing. She planned to be gone awhile."

"But why?" Kathleen whispered, stunned.

"I think you'll have to get that answer from Holly. She said that
Heather was upset this morning and they talked. She said Heather
was still upset when she left the house. That was the last time Holly
saw her."

Kathleen nodded, unaware of the motion. "Where is Holly
now?"

"In her room. Mattie's with her."

Kathleen turned to leave the room, but was stopped when
Earl pushed slowly to his feet and said, "Miss Kathleen, I'm
sorry. She must have slipped in when I went to the dining hall
for some lunch."

"I don't blame you, Earl." She went to him and reached out to
squeeze his weathered hand. "Heather's very clever. If she was
determined to go, she would have found a way to get around you."
She smiled gently. "That's not your fault."

Earl's fingers tightened around hers before he released her hand.
"You can be sure we'll find her for you," he vowed.

"I believe you will," she said before she turned and left the
room. She hurried up the stairs and down the hallway to the room
the girls shared. After a quick knock she pushed the door open.

Holly jumped up from where she was sitting on the edge of the bed next to Mattie and rushed to her mother. Kathleen opened her arms and gathered the trembling girl close.

"It's all my fault, Mom," she wept. "I'm the reason Heather ran away."

"Shhhhh," Kathleen said soothingly. "It'll be okay, honey. We'll find Heather and she'll be just fine."

But there was no consoling Holly. Kathleen met Mattie's worried eyes over the top of her daughter's blond head as the other woman rose to leave the room. Kathleen smiled her thanks before Mattie slipped out and closed the door. After a few minutes, Kathleen led Holly over to the bed and sat down there with her. She pulled a couple of tissues from the box on the night stand and pressed them into the girl's hand.

"Why don't you tell me what happened," she urged gently.

Holly straightened and made a valiant effort to stem the flow of tears. She looked over at her mother and drew in a shuddering breath. "I told Heather about Daddy," she managed to choke out.

Kathleen went very still as she watched her daughter closely. "What did you tell her about Daddy?" she asked carefully.

Holly swallowed hard and ducked her head. "I told her how he said ugly things to you. I told her. . . . I told her how he hurt you."

The shock that rammed into Kathleen carried the force of the proverbial ton of bricks. It wasn't possible that Holly knew. She couldn't know. Kathleen had always been so careful. The girls were never to know. But Holly's next words made her realize what a complete sham her cover-up had been.

"I could hear sometimes when he started in on you," she said, her voice low and strained. "And I could hear him the other night."

If Kathleen hadn't been sitting, she would have hit the floor. She couldn't even speak. But Holly didn't seem to notice. She was intent on her confession.

"Heather talked to Daddy this morning and was upset. He'd told her that he would let her come to Chicago to live, but you wouldn't allow it. I had to tell her that he was lying," she said simply, not even looking to her mother for confirmation of the lie. "She was so angry with you and it wasn't your fault. I had to tell her the truth." She paused and systematically shredded a tissue. "I had to tell her."

Kathleen's mind raced in circles, searching for a way to deal with all the emotions her daughter had just revealed. The magnitude of it was nearly overwhelming. "Holly. . . ." Her voice faltered as she tried to order her thoughts. Finally, she admitted softly, "I don't know what to say to you."

Holly looked over at her, blue eyes steady and calm. "Tell me no matter what he might threaten, that you won't let him hurt you again," she said simply.

Kathleen stared at her, hearing the plea behind the words. How long had this child been carrying the burden of her mother's fears? Any length of time was too long. Kathleen had never seen the truth until this moment. While completely convinced that she had been protecting her children all this time, it suddenly became crystal clear that she had actually done them more harm. While she had pretended that everything was okay, their whole lives had been reduced to nothing more than one big lie. How could she have been so blind?

She reached out to touch Holly's hair. "I can promise you right now that he'll never hurt me again," she promised. "Never, Holly."

A wan smile appeared briefly on the girl's face before she reached out to wrap her arms around her mother.

Thirteen

Cody paused on a high plateau and reached up to pull the collar of his jacket tighter around his neck. The thunderheads were moving in fast from the west. Within the last fifteen minutes the wind had picked up and the temperature had dropped several degrees. The air was sharp with the pungent scent of pine and the unmistakable essence of rain.

He'd gone farther than he'd originally planned and now it looked like he was going to have to ride hard to beat the storm home. It had been an incredibly stupid thing to do considering the way he felt. He suspected that his body temperature was on the rise again. He definitely knew that his head was once again thumping like a snare drum. Obviously, his body was reminding him that he'd pushed it. And now he faced the very real threat of getting soaked and further aggravating things.

He did have one other option. There was a line cabin about a mile to the west. He could find some shelter there until the worst of the storm passed and then head home. That would get him home long after dark, but at least he'd be dry.

Thunder rumbled in one low volley, causing the horse to shift restlessly beneath him. Taking the hint, he urged Lightning forward, deciding to hole up in the line cabin for a while.

An unexpected movement in a stand of pine trees to the west caught his eye and he reined the horse in. Watching intently, he expected to see a deer or antelope dart into the opening. He was startled to see a horse and rider break free of the trees and gallop at top speed across the meadow. Hardly more than a shadow in the fading light, he couldn't make out who it was. But it didn't matter. Whoever it was, they were headed toward a pretty rough stretch of mountainside. Nothing existed there except what nature had provided. Shelter would be next to impossible to find if the storm became as nasty as Cody suspected it would.

Swearing softly, he urged Lightning into motion again. The trail down the side of the mountain was well used and the horse maneuvered it with ease. Still, Cody saw that the other horse was closing the distance to the forest on the far side of the meadow. His goal was to intercept the mystery rider before he, or she, entered those trees.

Lightning took off like a shot when he hit solid ground, his sleek legs quickly eating up the distance. Within minutes they had closed in on their adversary. Cody's second shock of the past ten minutes came when he realized who he was chasing.

He yelled her name, and Heather shot a startled look over her shoulder. But instead of stopping as Cody expected, she urged her horse on harder. Cody swore again. What was it about the Hunter women that made them so adverse to accepting his instructions?

It took only a few more seconds for Lightning to overtake the smaller mare. Cody reached for the reins, but a small hand raked viciously across the back of his.

Surprise had him jerking back, but anger had him solving the problem neatly by leaning over and hauling the young rider completely off the back of the horse. Immediately, Heather began to kick and scream, and he fought hard to keep from dropping her as

Lightning slowed. They were still moving when she managed to squirm free of his hold and tumble to the ground.

With his mount finally under control, Cody turned back to check on his young opponent. To his amazement and fury the fall hadn't slowed her any. She was up and running toward her horse, hoping he was sure, to make another get-away.

Deciding he'd had enough, he slid off the back of the horse and started after her on foot. He brought her down with a flying tackle that would have winded most two-hundred pound football players. She, however, rolled away from him and began to scramble to her knees. He caught one of her ankles and was rewarded with a kick to his shoulder by the other booted foot. Grunting from the impact, he managed to capture both of her legs and pin them securely beneath one of his knees. Fighting with her hands, she sent his hat flying and caught his chin with a small fist before his fingers imprisoned her wrists. She screamed her frustration and then began to cry with such abandon that Cody could only stare at her in wonder.

He was breathing hard, gasping deep for air that seemed to be locked somewhere in the vicinity of his burning chest. Sweat beaded on his forehead and ran freely down his face and back. Fighting back a sudden wave of dizziness, he tried to calm himself and think rationally. Thunder echoed through the valley, vibrating the ground beneath them. Under the best of conditions, he was still nearly an hour from his ranch. He didn't know much about young females, but he suspected he had a very hysterical one on his hands now. He was way out of his league here and would have admitted it to anyone.

He looked down into Heather's face. Her eyes were swollen and tears glistened on her cheeks. Sobs racked her body and he could feel her tremble. Hoping that the fight had drained out of her, he eased his knee away and released her legs. When she didn't make any move to fight, he freed her hands. They dropped to her sides limply.

Sighing wearily, he sat back. Feeling as weak as a newborn colt, he managed to draw his knees up and rest his forehead there. He wasn't so certain that he wasn't about to pass out cold. As if from a distance far away, he heard her stir. Some instinct told him that she was about to make a break for it, but he couldn't have stopped her then to save his soul or her life. He was too damned weak to lift his head, much less chase her down again.

Vaguely, he wondered if it was thunder he heard or her riding away. Dammit, he couldn't let her go. Kathleen would never forgive him. Reaching down into the deepest part of himself, he found the strength to lift his head. One sluggish look told him what he already knew. Heather was gone.

He groaned softly and braced himself with one hand, fully intending to push himself to his feet. But the need to stand vanished as he tumbled headfirst into a black oblivion.

Kathleen was standing beside Jon, peering closely at the map he'd spread out on his desk. He pointed with the tip of his pencil, to where the ranch was located. "I've got the men fanning out from the ranch and in this direction," he said, indicating a northeasterly path. "If she went south, that would take her into Wolfe Creek. West would take her right to the face of those mountains. Northeast seems to be the only direction that makes sense. It'll take her right though the center of Washington land, and away from their ranch."

Thunder clapped sharply overhead and Kathleen jumped. Her eyes went instantly to the window where rain ran down the glass in one unbroken sheet. She folded her arms against her chest and focused her attention on the map. It didn't look like such a big area on paper. But she knew how deceiving the map was.

A loud pounding at the front door drew their attention. Jon started around his desk, but Mattie called out that she'd get it. A moment later, a dripping Gary Hunter stood in the doorway.

Kathleen felt Jon stiffen beside her. "I told you to stay the hell off my property," he snarled.

Kathleen placed a hand on his arm as he started forward. "I called him."

Jon's head snapped around. "For God's sake, why?"

Kathleen continued to stare at her ex-husband. "Because I wanted him here," she said simply.

Gary shot Jon a cocky grin as he came further into the room. "See, Graham," he jeered. "I had a personal invitation from the lady."

Jon could only stare at his sister in disbelief. Mattie slipped an arm around his waist in a show of support.

Gary ran a hand through his wet hair and gave Kathleen a dark look. "This is a God-awful night to drag me out, Kathleen. What's all this silly nonsense about Heather running away? How could you let that happen? Have you found her yet?"

Kathleen slowly crossed the room, never taking her eyes off him. When she was standing directly in front of him, she took a moment to study him closely. He was just a man. Not a supernatural being or a demon straight from hell. He was just a man made of flesh and bone. No more. No less. He had strengths, but he had weaknesses, too. Everyone did. Why hadn't she realized that sooner? What had she been afraid of all this time?

Without blinking, she lifted her hand and slapped him. The force of the blow had his head snapping sideways. The surprise of the action had him standing stock still. Slowly he turned his head and pinned her with eyes churning with a dangerous fury.

"If anything happens to my daughter," she said in a perfectly calm voice, "I will hold you personally responsible. I will ruin your life. I will bring charges against you so fast that your head will swim. And I will make sure you suffer."

He glared at her a long moment before emitting a derisive laugh. "Charges of what? You have no proof, no witnesses. No one would ever back up your ridiculous accusations."

"It doesn't matter. I will tell everything to anyone who will listen. I think talking to Jackie would be a good place to start. But it doesn't really matter where I start. By the time I finish talking, I will have cast enough doubt on you to make your most adoring allies hesitate to trust you."

Gary's eyes darted quickly to Jon before returning to her. "You're real brave when one of your protectors are near, aren't you, Kathleen," he chided. "Why don't we finish this discussion privately?"

"We both know you're physically stronger than me. We both know that you can hurt me. But I'm telling you right now that we're done playing your games. I want you out of my life and the girls' lives. You have manipulated me and lied to the girls about me for the last time. If Heather is okay, and you better pray she is, I want you to disappear from our lives for good. If you refuse, I'll start a ball rolling that will flatten you in no time at all."

"You're bluffing."

"Try me."

She continued to meet his gaze directly and for the first time in her life, she saw a flash of uncertainty in his eyes. A satisfied smile curved her lips. "Just try me, Gary. I'll enjoy taking you down."

Several long moments passed when the only sound heard was that transmitted by the storm—rain rushing down the windowpanes and thunder raging wildly. Kathleen didn't back down. She'd made a promise to Holly. She was through being a victim.

"Okay, Kathleen," Gary said smoothly "I agree to your terms. Not because you scare me. I don't believe you have what it takes to follow through with your threats. I agree because I lost interest in you years ago. You mean less than nothing to me." He paused to gauge her reaction to his words. When her features remained impassive, he added blandly, "I think you're overlooking one tiny point. If I disappear from your life, so does my financial support."

"Take it. I have no need of your blood money."

Briefly, his eyes narrowed threateningly and then a taunting smile curved his lips. "It's your call," he murmured. He held her gaze for another heartbeat before turning and striding swiftly from the room.

Kathleen heard the front door slam and felt as if every bone in her body melted. She grabbed back to balance herself on Jon's desk at the same instant his hand closed around her elbow. He turned her to face him.

"My God," he growled. "You must have nerves of steel."

She gave a shaky laugh. "Are you kidding? Right now they feel like nerves of cooked spaghetti."

Mattie frowned. "Do you think he'll leave you alone?"

Kathleen shook her head. "I really don't know. But I won't hesitate to follow through with my threats if he doesn't. He's taken all he's going to from me."

The shrill ring of the phone intruded into the silence, and Jon turned to reach for it. Kathleen walked over and sat down in one of the chairs across from his desk as he carried on a short conversation.

When he hung up the phone, he ran a hand through his hair before turning.

"What is it?" Mattie asked warily.

"That was Olan," Jon said quietly. "He and Jenny just got in a little while ago. He said that Cody left a message on their answering machine that he was going to check fences up on the northern border of their property. He expected to be back early. He's still not in. It appears that he's out in this weather, too."

"I thought you said he was sick," Kathleen said.

"I knew he was sick when he was here the other night," Mattie claimed. "Jon, why didn't you tell me he got worse?"

"Because Cody asked that I not send either of you Florence Nightingales over there." He paused looking from his sister to his wife, his expression instantly contrite. "Look, you two, Cody's a big boy. He had the flu and preferred to suffer alone. Okay? Don't blame it on me if he didn't want anyone fussing over him."

"Well, if he's sick, why would he go out to check fences?" Kathleen asked.

"I'm sure he must have been feeling up to the ride. He's not stupid. The fact that it's after dark and he's not back simply means that he got caught in the storm and probably took shelter in one of the line cabins up there. Cody's okay," Jon stressed. "This is his life, and he knows how to take care of himself. Maybe if we're real lucky, he will have run across Heather. If that's the case, then we can be sure that they'll both be okay."

Kathleen felt an uneasiness settle in the pit of her stomach. Her gaze was drawn to the windows. Lightning flickered, thunder rumbled, and rain poured down. And her daughter and the man she loved were both out there in it.

The gradual lighting of the gray morning indicated that dawn had arrived. The sun was obscured behind low lying clouds that looked as if they might hang around all day. It was still raining, not in the torrents that had lashed at the earth yesterday and during the night, but in a gentle steady rainfall.

Kathleen had managed to steal a couple of hours of sleep. With the first light of the morning, she'd dressed in a heavy sweatshirt and jeans and headed downstairs. She wasn't surprised to find that Jon was already up and talking with some of the wranglers. When he saw her hesitate in the doorway of his den, he waved her in.

"Heather's horse showed up at the stables some time during the night," he informed her. "None of the gear she took was on the horse, so that leads us to believe that she found shelter somewhere."

Kathleen nodded and willed herself to stay calm. "What about Cody?" she asked. "Did he make it home last night?"

"I don't know yet. I'll call Olan in a few minutes."

Kathleen sat down and waited while Jon went over last minute instructions with the men. After they had departed, he turned and looked at her. "We'll find her today," he assured her. With a weary sigh, he sat down and rubbed his hands over his face.

"Did you sleep at all?" she asked.

"A little." He stifled a yawn and reached across the desk for the phone. "I better call Olan."

He had just begun to punch in the number when the front door opened. He paused and looked up expectantly. When Olan's tall frame filled the doorway, Jon replaced the receiver.

"I was just calling you," he said, pushing to his feet.

"Cody didn't make it home last night," Olan said without preamble. "Lightning did."

Jon swore softly. "That's not good news."

"No," Olan agreed. "I don't even want to think about how Cody might have become separated from that horse. Something definitely isn't right." He shot a quick glance at Kathleen before adding quietly, "The rifle is missing from the saddle."

Kathleen saw the look that passed between the two men and was instantly alarmed by it. She came to her feet. "What are you thinking?" she demanded. "What do you think could have happened to him?"

"Honey, we really don't know," Jon soothed. "Let's don't borrow trouble."

"Well, you two look like you are," she pointed out.

"I'm taking the Jeep up to the north ridge," Olan said. "Cody's been up there before in the vehicle, so I know it can be done. If the rain hasn't made the trails impassable," he qualified.

"I'd like to go with you," Kathleen said. Again, she caught the look that passed between the two men. She turned to Jon. "I can't sit here all day and wait," she said evenly. "At least with Olan I'll feel like I'm actively doing something." She hesitated and looked from Jon to Olan. "It may be silly, but I have a gut feeling that if we find one of them we're going to find the other," she said quietly. "Please let me go with you."

"It'll be a rough ride," Olan warned.

"So is waiting here."

Fourteen

Cody fought to emerge from the black whirling waves that threatened to drag him under again. He didn't want to go back to the tormenting images that he knew awaited him there. He struggled to reach the dim light that beckoned just up ahead. Lead weights seemed to have settled on his eyelids. When he finally forced his eyes open it was to find himself under the sharp scrutiny of deep blue eyes.

Heather stared at him a long moment before an unsure smile flitted across her face. "Hi," she said softly. "You're finally awake."

He started to speak, but found his throat so dry he couldn't form the words. Immediately, she bent down and picked up a cup of water from the floor. He raised himself up on one elbow as she held the cup to his lips. One thirsty gulp drained it all. She retrieved the canteen and filled the cup again. Cody finished it off and laid back against the mattress. He closed his eyes a moment, fighting off the dizziness that swept over him.

"Thanks for coming back for me," he murmured. When she didn't immediately respond, his eyes drifted open. He met her guilty gaze and a weak smile lifted one corner of his mouth. "You did ride off and leave me, didn't you?"

Mutely, she nodded.

"Yeah, I thought you were a little put out with my presence," he said ruefully. "You want to tell me what's going on? I know what I was doing out in the storm. Why don't you tell me what you were doing?"

She sighed and leaned back in her chair. "I was being stupid," she admitted bluntly. "I'm sorry I fought you like I did. I was just angry and you were the only target I had. I'm sorry if I hurt you."

"I don't bruise easily." He studied her quizzically in the dim light. "What happened to upset you? Was it your dad?"

"Yeah," she murmured. "He told me that he didn't care if I went back to Chicago with him. But he said Mom wouldn't let me."

"He lied to you, Heather."

"I know." He saw the weary sadness in her eyes and hurt for her. "But I've been lying to myself, too. For a long, long time. I thought I was running away because of something Holly told me, but that's not true. I was running away from myself, from the person I've become."

"You're not such a bad person."

She shook her head and dropped her gaze to her hands in her lap. "I knew he was hurting Mom, but I closed it out. I pretended none of it was happening."

Cody felt the air leave his lungs and knew it had nothing to do with his physical illness. Was it possible that the girls had known all along what was going on between their parents? "How did he hurt her?" he asked hoarsely.

She was quiet for so long that he thought she might not answer at all. Finally, she drew in a ragged breath and said, "He was so mean to her. He said awful things to her. Sometimes you could hear him late at night. His voice and his words were so ugly that I just wanted to close them out. I didn't want to believe it was him saying those things." She shook her head and closed her eyes. "She never wanted us to know. She always acted like everything was normal and that's what I wanted to believe. But she couldn't always hide the facts. She couldn't always hide the pain."

He shifted slightly and reached out to touch Heather's hair. When she looked at him, he said softly, "Did he ever hurt you or Holly?"

Heather shook her head. "Not like Mom," she said thoughtfully. "He just was never there for us. I pretended that his work was so important he had to be away. But the truth is, we didn't matter enough to him. Only Kevin mattered to him."

"Your baby brother?"

Heather frowned. "How do you know that?"

"Your mother told me."

"She did?" She stared at him a long moment. "We never talked about Kevin after he died. I think it hurt too much for her to remember all that."

"It still hurts her," Cody said. "But she loved your brother very much."

"I know." A soft smile lit her face. "Kevin was born when Holly and I were ten. He was a beautiful baby. Daddy fussed over him all the time." Her smile faded. "One day Kevin didn't wake up from his nap. He just quit breathing while he was sleeping. It was nobody's fault. But Dad blamed Mom. I walked into the living room once where they were talking and I heard him say that he knew she had killed Kevin." Her voice dropped to a whisper. "I pretended I didn't hear. I pretended he never said it."

Cody pushed the blankets away and struggled to sit up. Anger was simmering in the pit of his stomach like a poisonous brew. He wanted just one fair shot at Gary Hunter. Damn the bastard anyway. What kind of man purposely set out to systematically destroy his wife and daughters?

"What are you doing?" Heather asked, reaching out a hand to his forearm to steady him.

"I can ride," he ground out, willing the world to settle around him. "We're only about an hour from my place."

"It's still raining, Cody. You can't go out in this weather. You're too sick. Besides. . . ."

At her hesitation, he cast her a curious look. "What?"

"The horses are gone," she admitted weakly. "I didn't have them tied securely and the storm spooked them. I'm sorry."

He leaned back against the wall and shook his head. It was just as well. He doubted that he could have made the ride anyway. But that didn't stop his insides from churning. He needed to see Kathleen. He needed to know what she was feeling. He needed to know if there was even a chance that she could love him.

"Could you get my shirt?" he asked.

Heather retrieved his shirt from the back of the chair where she'd hung it. It was still warm from the fire when she handed it to him.

"Thanks," he said, as he shrugged into it. He shot her a glance as he was buttoning it. "You did a great job with everything, Heather," he said sincerely. "Even if I'd made it to the cabin on my own, I don't know that I could have gotten a fire going before I passed out. I certainly couldn't have kept it going through the night. Don't worry about the horses. I'd wager that they've both found their way home by now. It's only a matter of time until someone finds us. I'm sure they've been looking for you already."

"Are you hungry?" she asked. "Its already after noon."

He seemed to be making a habit of losing large chunks of time lately. "I didn't realize I'd been out so long." He nodded toward the pot she had hanging over the fire. "What do you have heating?"

"I opened some beef stew that was in the cabinet. I've also got some bread that I packed. I've already eaten, but there's plenty for you."

He smiled slightly. "It sounds good. Could you fix me some?"

"Sure."

He watched as she moved around the cabin, dishing up the stew and then breaking him off a piece of bread from the French loaf on the table. He didn't want to think about Kathleen worrying about her daughter, but it appeared that the experience had brought a new maturity to Heather. If nothing else, it had forced her to face head on some issues in her life that had been ignored far too long.

She sat across from him as he dug into the simple meal. He could almost see the wheels turning in her head and wondered what she was thinking so hard about. Finally he set the empty plate aside and met her gaze.

"You're a good cook, too," he complimented.

He was rewarded by a true smile. "All I did was open a can. I could hardly mess it up."

Cody shrugged. "It was still good."

She dropped her hands to her lap. He waited. After a moment she said, "You did a lot of talking while you were running a fever."

"Did I? I hope I didn't say anything to embarrass you or myself."

"No." She lifted her head. "You talked about Mom."

Cody didn't dodge the direct look. "I'm not surprised. I kept dreaming about her," he said easily.

"You said you loved her."

"I do." He paused. "Does that bother you?"

"No. Have you told her that you love her?"

Cody shifted slightly until he was resting more comfortably against the wall. "Not yet. I intend to tell her as soon as I see her again."

Heather hesitated before saying, "You won't hurt her, will you?"

"Like your father, you mean?" At her nod, he shook his head. "Never like that, Heather. I promise." He swallowed hard and reached his hand out to her. Without hesitation, she placed hers within his. "I don't want her to hurt anymore, Heather. I think it's her turn to be happy for once."

Heather nodded. "She's been happier since she came here. I thought it was just Montana. But I guess you had something to do with it, too."

"I hope so."

"Me, too," she said softly.

"We need to head back, Kathleen," Olan said. "It's getting dark."

Kathleen blew out a frustrated breath as the vehicle bounced along the rough ground. The sun had finally made an appearance late in the afternoon but was now disappearing behind the mountains. The air was instantly cooler and Kathleen wished they could search in the dark. But she knew that was impossible. There were too many dangers. They would just have to resume the search early in the morning.

"I really thought we'd find them," she said quietly.

"Maybe someone else has found them," Olan offered hopefully.

"Maybe." Her reply lacked any enthusiasm.

"There's a plateau just up ahead. Let's take one last look from there with the binoculars. If we don't spot anything we'll call it a day."

Olan maneuvered over the flat land and came to a stop well away from the rocky cliff. Kathleen climbed out, the binoculars hanging around her neck. A light westerly breeze teased the tendrils of hair that had worked themselves loose from her ponytail during the day. She took a moment to look out over the scenery. Even under the current circumstances, she had to admire the beauty of the view before her. The terrain changed with the rise and fall of the land. The unforgiving mountains sloped downward, giving way to gently rolling hills and long flat valleys. The sky to the west was a blushing pink and long shadows stretched across the meadow below.

Sighing, she lifted the binoculars to her eyes and slowly began to scan the countryside. Olan was standing beside the Jeep watching her.

"Do you see anything?" he asked.

"No." She made a complete sweep of the area again. Nothing new revealed itself.

"Kathleen?"

The edge in Olan's voice instantly caught her attention. She turned to him curiously, noting the intensity of his expression. "What is it?" she asked.

"Do you smell wood smoke?"

Kathleen frowned and turned back to face the breeze. She waited and sniffed the air, but couldn't honestly say that she smelled anything but the pine trees nearby.

"Wait a minute," Olan said softly. He walked quickly around the front of the Jeep. "There used to be a line cabin in this area." He frowned and looked to the west and then the south. He turned back to the west. "It's that way," he announced. "A mile or so. I know I keep getting a whiff of wood smoke. Let's check it out."

Without questioning his hunch any further, Kathleen turned and sprinted back to the vehicle.

Heather was getting scared. Shortly after Cody had eaten he'd fallen back asleep. He'd been peaceful enough until about two hours ago. First the chills had set in and she'd built the fire up, almost to the point that she was uncomfortably warm. But as he'd grown more restless, his fever had shot back up. She kept trying to cool him off, but it seemed that he was sweating more now than he had last night. His breathing was shallow and labored, as if he was having trouble pulling in air.

She didn't know what else to do for him. Tears stung her eyes as she squeezed water out of the rag and then placed it against his flushed face. What if help didn't come in time? Night was falling, and she knew anyone searching for her would have to stop when it got too dark. It looked like she and Cody would spend another night in the small cabin. Looking at him now, she wasn't sure he'd survive another night. She pushed the frantic thought aside, warning herself not to become hysterical. She had to remain calm if she was going to be any good to Cody.

It was during one of these mental lectures that she thought she heard the sound of an engine. At first she thought it was an airplane and stopped to listen closely. But then she realized it was a vehicle. She dropped the cloth into the water and rushed to the door. In one smooth movement she pulled it open and barreled out into the twilight.

The sound of the engine was growing louder, but she could tell that it was still traveling well away from the cabin. It occurred to her that it could very easily pass them by. Through the stand of trees concealing the cabin, she could see the headlights of the vehicle drawing closer. With a frustrated cry, she began to run toward it. If she could reach the opening before they passed, she might be able to catch their attention.

Desperately she ran, falling once and scraping her hands and bruising her knees as she hit the rocky soil. She scrambled back to her feet and continued on. The vehicle was moving slowly, as if searching as it went. She plunged into the trees, pushing at branches with her hands and ignoring the ones that slapped her in the face. She stumbled into the clearing, breathing so hard her stomach clenched. To her dismay, the vehicle had passed her location, leaving only the eerie red glow of taillights to mock her.

"No!" she cried, tears rushing forward to drench her cheeks. She drew in one deep breath and screamed, "Stop! Come back!"

The red taillights blurred in the distance and she dropped to her knees, her sobs echoing in the stillness. It wasn't until the headlights were shining in her face that she realized they'd circled around and come back. Instantly she was on her feet and running toward them. The passenger door sprang open before the Jeep came to a complete stop, and suddenly her mother was there, her arms wrapping securely around her trembling body.

"Oh, God," Heather sobbed. "I thought you we're going to leave me."

"It's okay," Kathleen soothed. "You're safe now. Are you hurt? Let me look at you."

Kathleen drew back to peer at her daughter closely in the glow from the headlights. "You are hurt," she said, noting the scratches on her face and the blood on her hands.

"No," Heather said quickly. Olan came up beside them and she turned to him anxiously. "You've got to help Cody," she said urgently. "He's real sick."

"Show me where," Olan demanded. "Kathleen see if you can find a way to get the Jeep through those trees," he called as he started after Heather.

* * *

"Does the word pneumonia mean anything to you?" Jenny asked, bracing a hand on her hip as she glared down at her difficult patient.

"Yes," Cody snapped. "It means I'm damned tired of lying in bed."

They continued to glare at one another until Jenny was forced to look away. "Okay." She sighed heavily. "How about if we sit out on the patio for a while?"

He arched a brow. "How about if you get out of here and let me get dressed. I'm sick of this bed and this room. I promise I won't tire myself out," he added sarcastically.

"Cody, why are you so difficult? The doctor said. . . ."

"I don't give a damn about the doctor! He hasn't been confined to this bed."

"You never were a good patient, Cody," Brent Small chided as he ambled into the room. "I can hear you yelling all the way outside."

Jenny gave a heartfelt sigh of relief at the sight of the doctor. Without a backward glance she turned and hurried from the room, more than willing to turn Cody's care over to a professional.

"All I want is to get up, get dressed, and get on with my life," Cody said through clenched teeth. "Is that asking too much?"

The doctor gave a careless shrug. "I don't know. Let's see."

Cody endured the examination, already determined to overrule the old man if he recommended one more minute of bed rest. Any idiot could see that he was almost as good as new. It wasn't like he was planning to do anything extremely strenuous.

Of course, if he got his hands on Kathleen, he might reconsider that notion. She'd been conspicuously absent for the last week. She'd been there the day he'd come home from the hospital and he'd tried to talk to her, tried to tell her things she needed to know, things he needed to say. But she'd put him off, saying that they'd talk when he had his strength back. And then she'd disappeared.

Heather and Holly had been in and out several times. Jon and Mattie had been around. Even old Earl had stuck his head in one afternoon and stayed for a game of checkers. Kathleen was the only one who had stayed away. Cody couldn't decide if he was angry or terrified about her absence. All he knew was that he was tired of wondering what was going on in her mind.

"I think you might be able to get up and move around some," the doctor said easily. "Nothing strenuous, though. No horseback riding. No fence hole digging."

"I get the point," Cody returned tensely.

Brent packed his instruments into his bag and turned to pin his patient with a no-nonsense look. "Pay attention to what I'm telling you," he warned. "And pay attention to what your body tells you. You still need to take it easy. I don't have to remind you of how sick you were. Your lungs are still weak. Give them a break and don't push things."

"I promise to be good."

A wide grin added more lines to the doctor's aged features. "That'll be a first," he decided. At Cody's dark look, he chuckled. "If you do take it easy, I'd say you'll be back up to par in a week or so." He picked up his bag and headed for the door. "Let me know if you have any problems. I'll let Jenny know it's okay for you to be up."

The man had no more than cleared the doorway before Cody was up and searching for a pair of jeans. It was damned inconvenient not to be at home, but his father and Jenny had insisted that he recuperate in one of their spare bedrooms. If he had his way, which he was counting on, he would not be spending another night in this room. He was sleeping in his own bed tonight, in his own house.

He slipped into a shirt and quickly worked the buttons. Right now he had one priority: to find Kathleen and talk to her. It was time to put an end to all the questions spinning around in his head.

Cody was pleased to see the row of fresh gravel that ribboned away from the highway and back toward the museum. At least Kathleen had managed to get a little work done while he'd been laid up. Granted, he still wouldn't be much help, but they would eventually get everything done. The opening may have to be pushed back a week or two, but. . . .

His thoughts skidded to a halt as he cleared the stand of trees and got his first glimpse of the museum. Abruptly, he stopped the truck and just stared. The old colonial gleamed in the early afternoon sun with a fresh coat of white paint and shutters painted a silver gray. The grounds had been trimmed and were immaculate, with late summer flowers bordering the porch. An asphalt parking area had been poured to the south of the building and he counted five cars parked there. The tiny island in the center of the circular drive boasted a large sign that informed the visitor that they had just arrived at the Sara Ann Washington Museum of Western Art.

Cody shifted the truck into gear and continued along the drive. It appeared that Kathleen had been very busy these last few weeks. She obviously hadn't been sitting around waiting for his help. Maybe this explained why she hadn't been around to see him. She hadn't had the time.

He silently cursed himself for a fool as he climbed out of the truck and headed toward the museum. Would he have felt better if she'd sat around and waited for his every little suggestion? Probably his ego would have enjoyed it. But it wasn't his ego that was at stake here.

The outside had been a surprise, but the inside was stunning. He stepped into the entryway and stopped. The oak floors had been buffed until the grain in the wood stood out in sharp contrast. The same had been done with the banister skirting the curving staircase and balcony. The oak trim he'd been staining was finished and now adorning the doorways and windows.

Voices drifted down from upstairs, but none of them were Kathleen's. He stepped into the room on the right and found some of his father's paintings lining the perimeter of the room, as if she hadn't decided quite where she wanted them yet. He continued on, his footsteps echoing quietly, finding more of his father's work, and some that wasn't, in the other rooms.

It was in the last room that he found what he considered to be the greatest treasure of all. Kathleen sat on her knees on the floor, a clipboard on her lap, and a sea of quilts surrounding her. Every imaginable shade was there, almost assaulting the eye with the explosion of color. But Cody barely noticed. His attention was riveted on the woman as she absently tucked a loose strand of blond hair behind her ear and concentrated on what she was writing on the clipboard. A vivid turquoise blouse set off her tawny hair and disappeared inside the narrow waistband of her black dress slacks.

He wasn't prepared for the wave of love and desire that rocked him at just the sight of her. Suddenly all the impatience he'd felt trying to get to her vanished. He never wanted to push her into any corners. She'd been pushed around enough for one lifetime. He wanted nothing more than to share the rest of his life with her. But he already knew if it wasn't what she wanted, then he'd let her go. Somehow.

He knew the instant she felt his presence. He saw her shoulders tense, and she slowly lifted her head. When those blue-gray eyes met his, he saw a flash of confusion. But it was chased away by emotion so rich and pure it nearly took his breath away. She whispered his name as she pushed to her feet. And every fear that had tormented him for days died a certain death as she walked right into his arms.

He caught her close and buried his face in her silky hair. She wrapped her arms tightly around his neck as if afraid he might disappear. They stood that way a long time, content just to be together. When he finally drew back to look down into her face, he was surprised to see wet tears on her cheeks.

"You don't know how happy I am to see you here," she whispered, reaching up to caress his cheek.

He caught her hand in his and placed a kiss against her palm. "Did you miss me just a little?"

She gave a laugh that sounded awfully close to a sob. "I missed you a lot," she confessed. "If you ever scare me like that again. . . ." Her voice trailed off and he took the opportunity to drop a gentle kiss against her lips. But a light kiss was not enough for either of them. Her fingers tightened in his hair at the back of his head as his mouth came back for a second pass. He settled into the kiss with a near desperation that both surprised and thrilled. Kathleen stretched up toward him, opened to him and poured all of her feelings for him into it.

When they finally drew apart, she rested her head against his chest, listening to the accelerated thud of his heart. A frown creased her features and she lifted her head to gaze at him. "I'll bet you're supposed to take it easy and your heart is racing."

A wicked grin split his face and he dropped a quick kiss on her forehead. "Katie, if loving you kills me, I'll go a happy man."

Her frown deepened as true concern darkened her eyes. "Don't joke about it, Cody. I don't think you know how close you were to. . . ." Her voice broke, leaving her unable to say the word.

"Katie," he whispered, his hands framing her face. "I'm okay now. You don't have to worry about me anymore."

She turned away from him and walked to the window, her arms hugging herself to ward off a chill that radiated from the inside out. "I keep seeing you like we found you in the cabin," she said, her voice hollow. "I really thought we were going to lose you before we got you to the hospital."

"But you didn't." He came up behind her and wrapped his arms around her waist. She nestled back against him. "I was determined to make it just so I could apologize for all the stupid things I'd said to you. I am sorry, Katie. I pushed you when I should have been doing nothing more than offering support. I thought I knew a lot more than I actually did."

"You weren't so wrong," she said quietly. "I kept hearing your voice when I first faced Gary down. You had faith in me, when I had very little in myself. You saw a strength in me I never knew existed. I didn't think I could ever be strong enough to win against him."

"I still went about it all wrong." He sighed. "Jon told me what happened between you and Gary. I'm proud of you, Katie."

She closed her hand over his and lifted it to her lips. "Thank you," she murmured, her voice thick with unshed tears.

He stood for a moment and just held her, enjoying the weight of her body nestled close to his own. In a low voice he said, "Heather told me some things about your life with Gary."

"Poor Heather." Kathleen drew in a deep breath. "She was caught so neatly between the reality and illusion of our family life. It never occurred to me that I was hurting the girls by staying in the marriage and pretending. I always thought it would be worse for them if I broke away. I never considered that they knew as much as they did. We've started seeing a counselor in Bozeman, and I think we're going to be okay." She gave a soft laugh. "Actually, I know we're going to be okay. For the first time, none of us are keeping secrets. Already we're in better shape than we've ever been."

"You're going to be great, Katie. You've got two special daughters, and they're going to grow into two special women." He turned her in his arms until she was facing him. "Like their mother," he added, looking down into her face. "I love you. I knew it a long time ago, I just didn't have the courage to tell you. I didn't think it was fair to ask you to jump into another relationship so soon after freeing yourself from a bad marriage." He smiled and smoothed her hair back. "Now I'm not going to wait any longer. I love you, and I'd like to share the rest of my life with you as your friend, your lover, your partner."

Her smile trembled as tears threatened. "Heather and the nurses and doctors all told me how you kept saying that you loved me while you fought the fever. Whenever I was with you, you were deathly still. It seemed sometimes that you weren't even breathing. I'm glad to hear you say the words now, knowing you're not running a fever."

"I'm very lucid," he assured her. "I will be more than happy to declare my love every day from now on. Will you marry me, Katie?"

She hesitated, and he felt a chill of apprehension. "There's something you need to know before you make that offer."

He sensed the tension in her and felt his own increase in response. "What is it?"

Her gaze wavered and dropped away. "You need to know that I can never give you any children. A year after Kevin died I became ill and had to have a complete hysterectomy. I can never have any more babies."

The relief that rushed through him weakened his knees. He placed a finger under her chin and tilted her face up. "I love you," he stressed. "Children are never a guarantee in any marriage. I'll love your daughters like my own. Maybe we'll have lots of grandkids."

She stared up at him, her love in her eyes. "Are you sure?"

"You and your love is all I'm asking for." He smiled. "Will you marry me, Katie?"

"Yes." The answer was firm and without reservations. "I always told myself I'd never marry again. But I came to realize that I never knew love until you." She reached up and caressed his cheek. "I love you, Cody. Forever."

He swept her close and sealed the promise of their shared future with a kiss that promised to go on and on.

"I figured this is where I'd find the escaped patient."

Cody lifted his head and fixed his gaze on his father leaning in the doorway. He grinned. "I'm holding the best medicine in the world right here in my arms."

Olan chuckled. "I don't doubt it. Why don't you act like you've got some sense and ask her to become a part of our family?"

"You must be psychic. I just did that."

Kathleen turned and smiled at her future father-in-law. "At least this way if Cody gets sick again he'll have someone to take care of him, since he seems incapable of doing it himself," she teased.

Olan's eyes sparkled as he eyed the happy couple. "You'd better watch it, Kathleen," he warned. "If I know my son, he wouldn't be above feigning an illness just to keep you at his bedside."

"No way," Cody denied. "I don't want her at my bedside. I want her in my bed. There's a big difference."

"Stop it," Kathleen scolded, her cheeks heating. With a shake of her head she crossed back to where she'd left her work in the middle of the room. "If you two are going to hang around here, I'll have to put you to work."

"It looks to me that you've already put a few people to work around here," Cody commented. "I hardly recognized the place when I drove up."

"Actually, it was pretty amazing," Olan said. "Once you were out of the picture, all kinds of things started getting done."

Kathleen laughed softly and picked up her clipboard. "What happened was I put out the word that I needed help. What's amazing is how many people are interested in seeing this museum open. Wolfe Creek is full of talented and caring people who were more than ready to help me. This place will truly belong to the community."

Olan nodded his agreement. "As it should," he murmured.

"What are you doing with the quilts?" Cody asked.

"They're going to be a special display," she explained. "I thought it would be interesting if every month or so we featured a special exhibit of some kind. Quilting is a form of art that can be traced back all through American history. And look at all of these." She waved a hand around the room. "Not one alike, or even close. They're all wonderful."

Olan's smile was gentle as he looked at her. "Sara would have loved what you've done. Thank you."

She crossed to him, tears stinging her eyes. "Thank you for believing in me." She reached up to hug him.

"So when are you planning to open?" Cody asked.

"Three weeks," she announced, turning to him. "The invitations will be going out tomorrow."

"Do you think you might squeeze a wedding in sometime before the opening?" he asked casually.

"I might. Are you going to be up to any kind of a honeymoon?" she inquired smoothly.

Olan covered his chuckle with a cough and turned to leave the room. Cody's eyes narrowed as he crossed to her. His hands curved around her upper arms and slowly drew her closer. "I've been assured that another week of rest should put me back in top shape."

She nodded and arched a brow. "Then we'll get married in two weeks," she decided. "Just to be sure, of course."

"Thanks," he growled as he bent to capture her lips.

"And just to be on the safe side," she said, as she slipped away from him, "we'll practice abstinence until then."

His brows shot up. "Complete abstinence?" he asked incredulously.

"Complete." She reached up and gave him a quick kiss. "Come on." She caught his hand and pulled him toward the stack of quilts. "We've got a lot to do if we're going to squeeze a wedding and honeymoon in before opening. You can help me tag and record all these quilts." She handed him the clipboard.

"Okay," he conceded grudgingly. "But I get you all to myself for at least four solid days after we're married."

"If we get everything set up ahead of time, I don't see why we can't squeeze out five or six days."

"All right!" He looked like a kid who'd just won first prize in a contest. "Let's get started."

She mirrored his expression, knowing for certain that she'd just won the best prize—a prize that would last a lifetime. She'd finally found that special somewhere to call home.